TRAVELLING MAN

Lomax flicked open the pages of the paper, until he came to page 7. There was a photograph of himself, from two years ago, glaring ferociously at the camera. "Disgraced ex-policeman freed today," said the headline. "Former Drug Squad Detective Inspector, Alan Lomax, 37, is due to be released from Motram Prison this morning, after serving two years of his three year sentence.

"Lomax, a former Drugs Squad Officer, had been convicted of stealing £100,000 of police funds in an elaborately faked drugs heist. In spite of his strong denials of guilt, the missing money has never been recovered."

'Thanks, slob,' Lomax said, quietly under his breath. 'Just in case anyone in the world didn't know I was coming out today...'

TRAVELLING MAN

Peter James

Based on the Granada Television Series
'Travelling Man'

Written by Roger Marshall

A STAR BOOK
Published by
the Paperback Division of
W.H. ALLEN & Co. PLC

A Star Book
Published in 1984
by the Paperback Division of
W.H. Allen & Co. PLC
44 Hill Street, London W1X 8LB

Printed and bound in Great Britain by
Anchor Brendon Ltd, Tiptree, Essex

ISBN 0 352 31606 3

CHAPTER ONE

Lomax knew, as he walked out through the prison gates, that whatever else, he had been safe in there. He was not safe any more.

A tall man, with an athletic frame and dark hair cropped short, he wore an impassive expression set firmly on his face. Somewhere, from deep inside the mask, a hint of sadness seemed to be trying to escape.

He looked over his shoulder and gave a loveless glance at the sprawl of prefabricated bungalows, one of which had been his home for the past two years. Then, gripping his brown paper parcel tightly, he began to walk down the road, putting as much distance as he could between himself and Motram Prison.

It was a special day today; not just his release from jail, but the anniversary, the third anniversary, of the day he was arrested. July 4th. It was nine o'clock in the morning, and it was going to be a humdinger of a day. He walked down the country road towards the railway station which he had often passed in the prison van, keeping his policeman's eye out for anything that might send a signal of danger to his brain.

He wondered how alert he still was, after two years of fibreless food and not enough exercise. From the sweat that was already forming on his brow, after less than a quarter of a mile, he knew he was no longer fit. But fitness he could get back; that would be the easy part. How much else of his shattered life would remain? How much of that would he get back?

Jan had taken off; gone to Canada. The last letter he had

received from her, over a year ago, was brief and to the point. Steve, his fifteen-year-old son; where was he now? The respect of his parents: that was gone; his career in the police force: gone; and two of the best years of his life: gone. He had been arrested a week after his thirty-fourth birthday; still a young man then. Now, at thirty-seven, middle age was suddenly very close. And unless he acted pretty smartly, his chances of reaching it were not good. Not good at all.

He reached the tiny railway station, and the elderly ticket clerk looked him up and down from his booth. The only people who ever caught the 9.32 were released cons, and from his casual clothes and the brown parcel, he didn't need any further proof of his identity.

'London, second class,' said Lomax.

'Single or return?'

'Single.'

'Sure you don't want a return, just in case?' The man said, with a snide grin. 'Valid three months.'

'I'm not coming back,' said Lomax.

'Heard that before,' said the collector.

'Lucky you,' said Lomax.

'If I had a fiver for everyone who said they weren't coming back . . .'

Lomax picked the ticket off the counter and walked through to the deserted platform. He put down the parcel and sat on the seat; but the ticket collector wasn't finished.

'Thought you were going to London,' he called out.

Lomax looked round at him. 'That's the general idea. You're catching on fast.'

'Faster than you, John. You're on the wrong platform.'

Wearily Lomax got up and walked down the steps of the underpass. He was right, he knew, when he had thought that it wasn't going to be easy. At least in prison, he had belonged; one of a kind. It was harder, now that he was out; much harder. Bitterness began to well up inside him as he stepped out into the bright light on the far side of the station. When is a man guilty, he wondered? When he is convicted? Or when his family believe it? Or when he believes it himself?

6

No one had believed him. Not the judge. Not the jury. Not his wife. Not his parents. Only, perhaps Steve. And that was a big perhaps. Perhaps. Perhaps they were all right, and he was wrong. Perhaps he had taken the money after all, had had a mental relapse, and forgotten what he had done with it.

A train thundered into the station, and flashed past, sending a cooling blast of air around him. Snap out of it, he told himself. Snap out of it!

CHAPTER TWO

He noticed the car as soon as he came out of the tube station. A dark green Ford Sierra, with two men inside. He walked quickly down Fulham Broadway, keeping to the inside of the pavement, making the other pedestrians walk between him and the road. The fish and chip shop was still there, and so was the brass plaque on the doorway at the side of it. He pushed open the door and walked up the flight of stairs to the first floor. Painted on the glass door at the top of the stairs were the names Brierley, Clark and Alldis. He pushed it open and walked in. The receptionist, a new girl he did not recognise, looked up.

'I've come to see Mr. Brierley.'

'Do you have an appointment?'

'Tell him Mr. Lomax is here.'

'One moment, please, I'll see if he's in.'

'Don't worry. I'll see for myself.' Lomax walked past her, and pushed open the door behind her. He walked through into a spacious office. A short, unsmiling man, who looked dapper in spite of being considerably overweight, was standing with his back to Lomax, holding up a postage stamp with a pair of tweezers and inspecting it with a magnifying glass. 'British Guiana two cents,' he said, without looking round.

'Motram Open,' said Lomax, quietly. 'Two years.'

Brierley spun round, and the stamp fluttered to the ground. 'Good God!' he said.

Lomax stared at Norton Brierley, with contempt in his eyes. 'Making an honest living for a change, are you,

8

Brierley? Or ripping off another client?'

'Max! Good to see you – er – one moment.' Brierley bent down, picked up the stamp and put it on the desk.

'The office got smaller – or have you just got fatter?' said Lomax.

Brierley held out his hand. 'Good to see you, Max.'

'Top name on the door. What happened to Clark and Alldis? Get them put inside too?'

Brierley winced. 'Bought them out, as a matter of fact.' He smiled, nervously. 'You look good.'

'I looked better two years ago.' Lomax walked around the office. Idly, he began to flick through a stack of files on a shelf.

'Judge was lenient, it could have been a lot worse,' said Brierley. 'How was the food?'

'How was the food?' said Lomax incredulously. 'It wasn't a hotel. People didn't come in clutching their guide books.'

'Okay, okay. I heard prison food was getting better, that's all. Heard you even get a choice these days.'

'You do. Take it or leave it.'

Lomax walked over to the window and looked down at the Broadway. The green Sierra was parked a few yards back up the road.

'Drop of malt, Max. Got a rather nice Glenlivet – er, duty free, of course.'

'Death duty?'

Brierley flushed, and walked over to a cocktail cabinet.

'I don't drink in the daytime, and I'm in a hurry. Just tell me how I stand.'

'Come on, Max, what's the hurry. Three years –' he paused and pulled two glasses out of the cabinet. 'No – you had full remission, didn't you – twelve months – yes, two years inside. That merits a drink, Max.'

'I don't want a drink. I just want my statement – and my cheque.'

Brierley carefully set the two glasses down, and began to unscrew the cap of the bottle. Lomax suddenly snatched the bottle out of his hand, and screwed the top back on firmly.

'You're in a strange mood, Max.'

'Prison tends to blunt the social graces.'

'End of the week. Give me an address.'

'Now,' said Lomax, raising his voice. 'Now.'

Brierley walked over to a battered filing cabinet, and pulled out a file. He stood where he was and looked inside it. 'We used the best, Max. Top wig 'n' gown.'

'Fat lot of good that did me.'

'And Jan screwed you rotten. Bloody divorce judge was senile.'

'How much?'

'We sold the house, the furniture, paid off the mortgage, got rid of the car –'

'The boat?'

'No. Kept that – you told me to keep that.'

'How much is left?'

'There was Jan's air fare to Canada.'

'How much?' Lomax shouted, suddenly.

Brierley stared nervously at Lomax, and raising his forefinger, he pushed the tip of his nose first one way and then the other. 'Six grand and change.'

Lomax stared at him in disbelief, and sat down heavily on a chair. He stared down at the carpet. 'Six?'

'I'm afraid so.'

'Christ.'

'Want that malt now?'

Lomax stared up at him, bitterly. 'I thought there'd be fifteen, maybe even twenty.' He paused. 'What about Steve? Any news?'

'Not a dicky. Ran the ads as you told me. Every other day for a month. That wasn't cheap.'

'Fifteen-year-old boys don't just disappear.'

'He could be anywhere. Might have gone to Canada.'

'Never. They weren't that close. Jan never forgave him for being the one that lived. He wouldn't leave England, in any event. Loved the canals too much.'

'They have canals in Canada, Max. Ever heard of the St. Lawrence Seaway?'

'Iced in half the year.' Lomax looked out of the window again. 'Write the cheque out.' He watched Brierley pull his massive cheque book out of a drawer, and thought, for a fleeting moment, he had detected a trace of guilt cross the solicitor's face; but only the merest trace.

Brierley blotted the ink carefully.

'Where you heading for, Max?'

Lomax looked down out of the window at the Sierra. Brierley tore the cheque out of the book and handed it to him.

Lomax scanned it briefly, folded it and put it in the back pocket of his trousers, then turned and began to walk towards the door.

'Where are you heading for, Max?'

Lomax reached the door and opened it, without answering.

'Where shall I send the statement?' said Brierley. He paused. 'What shall I tell anyone if they want to get in touch with you, Max?'

'Tell them you don't represent me any more.' He slammed the door shut behind him, walked across the tiny reception hall, and into the lavatory.

He locked the door carefully, then pushed open the frosted glass window. There was a drop of about sixteen feet down into the rear yard. Lomax studied it carefully, then put his hand out and tested the strength of the pipe that ran from the floor above down into the drain. He hauled himself out of the window, and slid down the pipe into the yard. He climbed a fence, and dropped into a blaze of tulips. An old woman stormed out of the rear door of the house. ''Ere,' she said. 'What the hell do you think –?'

'My tennis ball,' said Lomax. 'I think it landed in this flower bed.'

'Clear off.'

'Well –' he smiled nervously. She looked very irate. 'If you find it – please throw it back –'

He ran past her, through the door into her house. He sprinted through the house, narrowly missing a startled cat, and hurled himself out of the front door, into a quiet back street.

Almost immediately, he heard the rattle of a diesel, and saw an empty taxi coming towards him. He flagged it down, and climbed in; he put his parcel on the seat beside him, and lay back. From the smell of the rich cologne which lingered around him, a woman had been in the taxi before him. For a few moments he wondered what she looked like. He imagined a mass of tumbling hair; expensive clothes; yes; she smelt like an expensive woman. It had been a long time, he thought, wistfully.

'Where to, mate?'

The cabbie's words jolted him. He was so used to prison routine, he realised, so used to everything being organised, planned, done; he had forgotten that in the outside world, cab drivers needed to be told where to go.

'115 Hazledene Avenue.'

'You could walk that from here,' said the cabbie.

Lomax looked over his shoulder out of the rear window. The road behind was empty. 'Expect I could,' said Lomax. 'But I rather fancy the scenic route.'

The house hadn't changed much, except for the flower beds in the front garden, which he had once spent hours tending, and which were now growing unkempt turf. Once, this had been home. Now it was just another tatty modern box. Had he really lived out fourteen years of his life in this house, in this street? Somewhere, further down the street, he heard an accordion playing. A squeeze-box, they called them in the States, he thought to himself, for no particular reason. It was an oom-pah-pah tune, better suited to a Bavarian tavern than a quiet backwash of Fulham, but it added an incongruous tang of jollity to the morning, a fragment of cheer to the depressing box of memories that stood in front of him. He thought back, to the early days of their marriage. Surely they were happy? he thought. He remembered Jan's fresh young face, her blue eyes that always looked at him with such trust, and he remembered the last time he had seen her, after the trial, when she had come to visit him in prison, with her skin dulled, and her eyes full of contempt. What had hurt him most was that she had cut her hair short. He had always liked it long, always insisted she kept it long. Cutting it had almost been an act of defiance; the final snub. He turned away, walked three houses up the street, and rang the doorbell.

A tall girl, pretty, but sloppily dressed, with a forelock of brown hair that slanted down her forehead, opened the door. Her face lit up when she saw Lomax, but behind the smile, he detected a hint of uneasiness.

'Max!' She threw her arms around him, and gave him a long kiss on the lips. 'You look wonderful.'

'So do you, Chrissie.'

'I think you've been having us all on. You've been on a bloody two-year cruise!'

Lomax smiled. 'How are you?'

'Fine. Fine.'

'How's Dave? The kids?'

'Fine. Everyone's well. We were wondering when you would be coming out. Tried to work it out. I found out about an hour ago.' Her face dropped.

'An hour ago? How?'

She jerked her thumb over her shoulder. Lomax instinctively took a step back, but the man had already come into the hall.

'Well well well, if it isn't the old prodigal son.'

Lomax glared at the man. 'I thought Fleet Street buried its dead,' he said.

The man gave him a wry smile.

'Robinson, isn't it?'

'Still retained your policeman's memory.'

'And you've still retained your knack of getting under my skin.' He glared at the ageing reporter, nattily dressed, and, as always, sporting a bow tie. His hands were too delicate, his face too well nourished. He always looked to Lomax as if he should have been an arts critic, rather than a crime hack. He turned to Chrissie. 'How'd he weasel his way in here?'

'He said he had an appointment with you.'

Lomax glared at him again. 'Who'd you make it with? My secretary?'

Robinson smiled. 'Very witty. You should go inside more often. It's improved your sense of humour no end.'

'I also learned a few conjuring tricks.'

'Oh yes?'

'Yeah. How to make fat reporters disappear.'

'Don't worry, Lomax. I'm not staying long.'

'You must be psychic.'

Robinson smiled, then stood, silently.

'So what do you want? No good stories around? Scraped the barrel and found my name at the bottom?'

'On the contrary, Lomax, you're at the top of the pile. Fresh out today. One hundred grand doesn't just disappear.'

'Doesn't it? I can give you the name of a solicitor who'd have no trouble at all losing that kind of money.'

'Come on Lomax. You might as well tell me the truth now. You've done your stretch. They can't do you again for it. Er – I've been told I could make it worth your while.'

'If you want the truth, go ask for the court records. Look up what I said. That was the truth.'

'One hundred grand in used folding. This story could be worth another five to you. You can travel a long way in life on a hundred and five grand.'

Lomax looked at him wearily. 'I don't know where the money is. I didn't know then, and banged up in a cell hasn't exactly given me much time for treasure hunting.'

'So you still reckon you were fitted up?'

'I was fitted up.'

Lomax sighed; it was old ground.

'Why?' said Robinson.

'They needed a patsy. My face fitted.'

'Come on, Lomax. Give us a lead. A few names.' He dug his hand into his jacket and pulled out a crumpled issue of his paper. 'Look – I wrote you a nice "Welcome Home". Page seven.'

'Why don't you pay for me to have a sex change – then you

'could put me on page three.'

'Word around Fleet Street is you'd better change your face. And your name. Otherwise I wouldn't bother taking out any magazine subscriptions, or buying any long novels, if I were you.'

'I suppose you've already written the obituary.'

Robinson smiled, slowly. 'Don't flatter yourself, Lomax.'

Lomax jerked forwards, grabbed Robinson by the wide lapels of his jacket, spun him around, and walked him backwards out of the door. As soon as he was clear of the step, he kicked away both his legs, and watched him fall backwards on to the pavement. 'Why don't you stay down there, Robinson,' he said. 'In the gutter. That's the right place for your office.' He slammed the door shut on him.

Chrissie turned to him. 'I'm sorry, Max.'

'Not your fault.'

'Come on, I'll make you a cuppa – or would you like something stronger –?'

Lomax followed her through into the kitchen. 'Coffee would be fine. Prison gets you out of the habit of drinking.'

It was strange being back in this house again, he thought. Chrissie and Dave had been their closest friends. Apart from the one visit from Jan, they had been the only people to visit him in jail the whole time he was there. They waded through the debris of kids' toys, and it calmed Lomax down, seeing the normality that was still able to survive in a world that otherwise, for him, had gone madder than he could ever have believed.

Chrissie began to fill the kettle.

'Did Jan talk much – about –?'

Chrissie nodded. She plugged in the kettle and switched it on. 'Took it very badly. If she hadn't gone away I think she'd have cracked.'

'At least she had a choice,' said Lomax, with a trace of bitterness.

'Still no sugar?'

Lomax smiled. 'Prison did a lot of things to me. But it didn't make me take sugar.'

15

'How was it?'

'How?'

She nodded, spooning coffee into the cup. 'Was it hell?'

Lomax stared out through the window into the rear garden. He looked at the neat stripes on the short lawn. 'The lawn looks good. Who cuts it?'

'Dave.'

'Are those begonias?'

'Yes. Pretty, aren't they.'

'Yes, it was hell.' He listened to the sound of the kettle beginning to steam. 'Why Canada?'

'She's got some relatives out there, hasn't she?'

'Not very close. Was there a fellah?'

'If there was, she kept it damned quiet. No, I don't think so.' She poured the coffee, and took a milk bottle out of the fridge.

'When did you last hear from Steve?'

'About a year ago. There was a reverse-charge call from Bletchley.'

'Bletchley? Grand Union Canal.'

'Grand Union?'

'Canals are in his blood. Like me. What did he say?'

'Nothing. I accepted the call and he hung up. Or was cut off. I don't know which. He never called back.'

Lomax sat down at the kitchen table, and tipped some milk into his coffee.

'What are you going to do now, Max?'

'I'm going to find my son and I'm going to clear my name.'

'And then?' she smiled.

'I never could plan too far ahead. Maybe I should have learned to, a long time ago.' He paused. 'I'm not going to tell you where I'm going to go – for your own safety. I'll call you from time to time, in case there are any messages.'

'My safety?'

'You, Dave, the kids. I'm flavour of the month at the moment. I've a feeling one or two people might be rather interested in me; and not just newspaper reporters.'

'You can stay here. We're not afraid.'

'Thanks. But I can't spend my life in hiding.' He smiled, and looked at his watch. 'And at the moment, I shouldn't spend too long in any one spot.'

'I've a couple of cases of your things. I'll get them – they're upstairs.'

He smiled. 'Thanks,' he said, as she walked out of the room. He took a sip of the hot coffee, then flicked open the pages of Robinson's paper, until he came to page 7. There was a photograph of himself, from two years ago, glaring ferociously at the camera. '**Disgraced ex-policeman freed today,**' said the headline. '**Former Drug Squad Detective Inspector, Alan Lomax, 37, is due to be released from Motram Prison this morning, after serving two years of his three year sentence.**

Lomax, a former Drugs Squad Officer, had been convicted of stealing £100,000 of police funds in an elaborately faked drugs heist. In spite of his strong denials of his guilt, the missing money has never been recovered.'

'Thanks, slob,' he said, quietly under his breath. 'Just in case anyone in the world didn't know I was coming out today . . .'

Chrissie came into the kitchen carrying a battered fibre-glass suitcase and a bulging Cathay Pacific grip bag. 'I don't know what's in them, but they're heavy enough.'

'No doubt everything that Jan decided she could live without.' He picked up the Cathay Pacific bag. 'That brings back a few memories. Drugs case in Hong Kong. The only perk I ever had.'

'Hong Kong or the bag?' smiled Chrissie.

He grinned. 'Not much to show for thirty-seven years, is it?' He unclipped the suitcase, and lifted the lid. He pulled out a single dulled brown shoe, and had a further rummage in the contents. 'Clothes; a few books.' He paused, and smiled sadly. 'Look – a ship's porthole!' He pulled it out. 'Got that diving on a wreck, once.' He dropped it back in the case. He stood, staring down.

'Don't get depressed.'

'I don't. I get gloomy. Maudlin. Sentimental. Lonely. But

I never get depressed.'

Chrissie laughed. 'We've missed you. A lot. Who knows. Maybe one day you and Jan'll get back together, Steve'll come back, and you'll buy a house, just down the road. Be like it was before. Who knows?'

'Yes,' said Lomax. 'Who knows?'

He turned and watched her smiling face, watched her blow one more kiss, before she shut the door. He put the heavy case on the pavement, and adjusted his grip on the handle. When he looked up, the green Sierra had pulled up in front of him. His eyes darted, left, right, searching for the best direction to run, the most obstacles, the hardest place for a car, the most places to duck and hide. The back door opened, and the burly figure of Detective Inspector Sullivan climbed out, a trifle too sprightly for his size, thought Lomax.

'Well, well, well,' said Sullivan. He sniffed hard, a couple of times and looked about him, before looking back at Lomax. 'Well, well, well, what do we have here?' He sniffed hard again.

'We have the genie – and I didn't even rub a lamp,' said Lomax.

Sullivan sniffed hard again. 'I do believe I smell bent copper.'

Lomax stared hard at him, then jerked his finger at the car door. 'Why don't you shut the door, keep the smell in?' Lomax sensed someone standing behind him. He glanced over his shoulder, and saw a plain-clothes sergeant he vaguely recognised. His path was blocked in both directions.

'The "Keep-Out" signs,' said Sullivan. 'Didn't you notice them? Big enough, aren't they, Sarge? Clear enough, aren't they, Sarge? – or should we have pinned a few bank notes to them?'

'They're big enough,' said the sergeant.

'Got a nice clean patch here, Lomax,' said Sullivan. 'Wouldn't want your muddy boots making it dirty.'

'Well, you can relax, because I'm not staying.'

18

'Well, that's a bit of good news. Isn't that, Sarge? Good news, eh?'

The sergeant nodded. 'Yes, Chief. Very good news.'

'We don't like bent coppers around here. Give good ones a bad name. Understand my drift, Lomax.'

'You must have been having English lessons, Sullivan. Your vocabulary's got wider since I last saw you.'

Sullivan eyed him, slowly, up and down. 'Got a message for you from the Commissioner. Wonders if he could have his money back?'

'I didn't take the money.'

Sullivan feigned surprise. 'No? Really? Well, that's funny, isn't it, Sarge. We could have sworn you had the money. Couldn't we, Sarge?'

'Certainly could,' said the sergeant.

'You ever considered emigrating, Lomax?'

'Ex-cons aren't exactly welcome in most countries,' said Lomax.

'Strange,' said Sullivan. 'I wonder why. Perhaps you could start a little sub-post office – somewhere a long way away?'

'That would suit him,' said the sergeant. 'He's used to looking out from behind bars.'

'Yes. Very appropriate. But then again, on second thoughts, no good.'

The sergeant looked at him. 'Why not, Chief?'

'Ex-cons can't run post offices.' He paused, thoughtfully. 'Have to settle for a boozer, Lomax.'

'Expect the local bill would oppose his licence,' said the sergeant.

Sullivan gave Lomax a large grin. 'Get the drift, Lomax? There won't be a second-hand dog licence with your name on it.'

'Let me know when you've finished,' said Lomax, giving him a sweet smile.

'You'll know when I'm finished, Lomax. You'll know.' He pointed a finger down the road. 'On yer bike.' Sullivan turned and began to climb back into the car. The sergeant followed.

Lomax turned away, then looked back. 'Sullivan,' he shouted out. 'Next time you want to give me a lecture, make an appointment, first.'

'There won't be a next time, Lomax,' said Sullivan.

CHAPTER THREE

It was late that afternoon when the taxi dropped Lomax at the small marina on the Grand Union Canal. He picked up the suitcase and the holdall, and walked in through the gate. Nothing had changed, but nothing ever did in boat-yards; one upturned rotting hull looks much like another, he thought; one unpainted river boat on a cradle much like another. The petrol pump was there, the diesel pump, the rusting gantry, the air a heady cocktail of the smell of diesel, mud and putrid fish, and always, from somewhere in the background, the whine of a drill.

'Well, I'll be damned,' said a booming cheerful voice. 'If it isn't the man time forgot!'

Jack Spurling, the marina owner, a wiry man in baggy denims and a red baseball cap, hurried over and pumped Lomax's hand. 'Good to see you. My God, it's good to see you.' He stood back, and examined Lomax. 'You've got that damned London pallor, other than that you look fine.'

'You don't look too bad yourself, old timer.'

'I don't want any cheek from you. Last time I saw you, you said: "See you in a fortnight." Some fortnight!'

'Traffic was bad,' grinned Lomax.

'Two years, just over,' said Spurling. 'I'm sorry – you know – about all your problems.'

'Thanks, Jack.'

'I want you to know, doesn't make any difference to me.'

'Thanks,' said Lomax. 'I appreciate that.' He paused. 'How's Frankie?'

'Fighting fit.'

Lomax looked relieved, and nodded over to the water. 'She still afloat?'

'Do you pay me to look after her or sink her?'

Lomax grinned.

'Come on, I'll pipe you aboard – just in case your crew's forgotten who you are.'

Lomax felt a tremendous sense of belonging, of homecoming, as he walked down the pontoon, and saw the familiar red, green and white paint of his beloved narrow boat, *Harmony*. He jumped on board. Spurling passed him the suitcase, then followed him.

'What do you think?' said Spurling.

'I'm impressed,' said Lomax. 'You've kept her better than I ever did.'

He unlocked the cabin door. 'Bloody hell – you've varnished the inside.' He paused, looked around anxiously for a moment, then breathed a sigh of relief. 'Frankie!' he shouted out. 'Frankie! I'm home. Remember me? Your old man?' Like an excited child, Lomax hurried down the narrow steps, and into the tiny galley where the budgerigar cage was hanging. He stuck his nose against the bars. 'Hello, boy, how you doing?'

The budgerigar eyed him curiously.

'You didn't reckon I was guilty, did you?' He lifted his finger up, and poked it through the bars. The bird studied it thoughtfully. 'You were the only one that stood by me – at least, the only member of my family that did.'

Suddenly, as if its memory clarified, the budgerigar gently nibbled his finger, and then began to chirp excitedly, and flap around its cage.

'All right, old boy, all right. I'm home now. I'm not going away any more. Ever,' he suddenly said, emphatically. He turned to Jack. 'Has he been well behaved?'

'Good as gold. I've fed him and watered him every day. Matter of fact I had him in my office most of the time, so he wouldn't get lonely.'

'Francis Albert,' said Lomax. He smiled ruefully at Jack. 'The only bird I never fell out with.'

The cheer fell for a moment from the marina owner's face as he sensed Lomax's sadness. 'I was sorry to hear about you and Jan.'

'She told you?'

'Drove up, autumn some time. Said she wanted to collect some things.'

''Fraid it was on the cards for a long time. Coppers are difficult to live with. Cons are even harder. How about Steve?'

'I've had my spies out, as you know. Not much to report, I'm afraid. Last I heard he was employed by a haulage firm out by Worcester. Adams.'

'Thanks. I'll pootle up that way.'

'That was some months ago.'

'I'm in no hurry. One thing about the nick. Kills your appetite for hurrying. I'll work my way around, slowly. Ask. He'll be somewhere on the canals.'

'Big place, the canals.'

Lomax smiled. 'Only about two thousand miles. I'll just have to cover them.' He walked on through the saloon, looking carefully around. He opened a cupboard. It was full of cans and bottles. 'Bloody hell, Jack – what's this? Aladdin's cave?'

'Thought you might be a bit peckish – and thirsty.'

'Thank you. How much do I owe you – for this and the – er – last two years?'

Jack smilingly pulled a thick brown envelope from his pocket. 'Nothing. I owe you.'

'What do you mean?'

Jack patted the envelope, and handed it to Lomax. 'There's about seven hundred in there.'

'Seven hundred?'

'I hired her out a few times. Carefully, mind you. No gongoozlers.' He smiled again. 'Seemed silly not to cover the mooring costs.'

'Thank you.'

Jack looked at his watch. 'Better get back to the office – I'm expecting a phone call.'

23

They shook hands.

'When are you off?'

'Right away,' said Lomax.

'I thought you weren't in a hurry?'

'So did I. But now I'm here, I'm already itching to get moving; always happens to me on the canals.'

Spurling smiled. 'Happens to most people. Good luck.'

'Thank you, Jack. And thanks for looking after her – and Frankie. I'll give you a call every few days – but just do me one favour – if anyone comes asking for me, don't tell them you've seen me.'

'Someone after you?'

'It's possible.'

'If you need anything. Anything at all. You call.'

'Thanks,' said Lomax. 'I'll remember that.'

CHAPTER FOUR

The man in the blue boiler suit pinched his nostrils together, then carefully investigated the roof of his mouth with his index finger. All the time he kept his eye on the photograph Lomax held in front of him. Suddenly, Lomax jumped, as a tremendous roar erupted behind him. He realised that, in spite of the good night's sleep he had had, moored to a quiet bank, his nerves were no longer as calm as they had once been. He turned around for a moment, and watched the coal surging down the shute on to the waiting barge.

'Yes, I do remember him. Nice kid,' said the man. 'But he wasn't called Steve.'

'You sure?'

'Aye.' He called out to one of his mates. 'Hey, Jim, come here.'

An angular man, with his skin pulled tight over his jawbone, lolled over, and inspected the photograph. 'That's young Ray. Ray Barlow. Remember him well enough. Good lad, he were.'

'Are you certain he was called Ray?' said Lomax. 'Not Steve?'

'Haven't had no Steve here. Not this yard. Not since old Steve Elks; that were ten year ago.'

'When did the kid leave?'

"Bout six months ago,' said the first man.

'No – it were ten month. Last summer. I know it were last summer. It were before I took my holiday. I remember. He were going to cover for me while I were on holiday, and then he told me he'd been sacked, because he didn't have no union

25

card. Some of the younger ones here threatening problems, you see. Aye. Ten months. I'd swear it.'

'Any idea where he went?' said Lomax.

'I told him to try Les Page's marina – at Lymm. They often take casuals.'

'Thanks,' said Lomax. 'I'll try there.'

Lomax walked thoughtfully back to *Harmony*. The network of canals was vast. But some day, surely, he would catch up with Steve. He wondered what would happen if he did find him. Would it be a happy reunion, or was Steve not only running away from Jan, but from him as well?

He unhitched the mooring ropes, and stepped on board. He leaned forward and pressed the starter. The engine rattled, missed a beat, then continued to rattle. He held it in until the rattle became constant, then released it, and the rattle settled down into the familiar chugging that was as much a part of the canals as the lapping of water. He steered out into mid-canal, and eased the throttle back slightly. He gave a wide berth to an elderly man who sat on the river bank, twine looped around his index finger, eyes riveted on a tiny yellow and white float that sat, at a slightly drunken angle, in the water in front of him.

He passed a massive red brick factory, then, as the canal curved to the left, he came to one of the kind of stretches that he loved the most: dead straight for miles ahead, with open fields on either side. The sight of the long canal ahead, and the open countryside, always gave him an intense feeling of freedom. He really began to feel that he was beginning to unwind. He congratulated himself on surviving so far. Not that it had been difficult; no one had come for him; yet. But it had only been a few days; early days, he knew; very early.

A splash of rain interrupted his thoughts, and he looked up at the darkening sky. He reached through the cabin door, and tugged out his oilskin coat. It smelt dank and musty as he slipped it on. Instinctively, he dug his hands into his pockets. There was a dirty handkerchief; some rusty keys – what they fitted he had long forgotten – and a withered conker on a string. The rain began to pour down heavily. He held the conker in his hand. Steve's pride, he remembered. A one hundred and forty-niner. Or was it a two hundred and forty-niner? He held the string and twirled it around. Suddenly, the string slipped out of his wet grip, and the conker sailed out over the water, and dropped down into his wake. He smiled sadly. Maybe Steve had another conker by now. Maybe he didn't play with conkers any more.

The rain stopped and the sky began to clear, as he tied up on the towpath in the centre of Lymm. It wasn't until he had locked up that he noticed the blonde-haired girl on the small red and yellow narrow-boat alongside him, hanging up laundry on her line.

'Do you know where Les Page's marina is?'

'You've just passed it,' she said cheerily. 'A couple of hundred yards that way.'

'Thanks,' he said.

'You're welcome.' She gave him a long smile.

He turned and walked back, past the·Lymm Cruising Club, kicking himself for not picking up on her smile, not chatting her up. Two years in prison and he'd lost the knack, he thought wryly.

He walked past a row of stone cottages, and then came to the narrow creek leading up to the marina. It wasn't hard to miss. The marina itself was brand new, and very smart. A red Porsche was parked outside a prefab office. He walked over and went in.

A woman in her late thirties sat behind the desk. Her clothes were casual but expensive, and her long peroxided hair was a mess. With less-sloppily applied make-up and a decent hairstyle, she could have been quite an attractive woman, thought Lomax. He smiled at her, and she nodded back.

'I know your face,' she said. 'Seen you around before, haven't I?'

'I know yours too – Les Page's wife, aren't you?'

'That's right.'

'You used to have a different marina – further on past Lymm?'

'Yes. This is new. Just opened this year.'

Somewhere in the distance, Lomax heard the roar of a motorcycle. He heard it slow down and stop.

'I'm afraid I can't remember your name,' she said.

Lomax studied her for a moment. Something about the way she sounded, as if she had a cold, the dry cough.

'Lomax,' he said.

The cough again. 'Lomax,' she echoed, twitchily. 'Lomax.' She sniffed. 'Difficult to remember names,' she smiled nervously. 'See so many faces during the summer.'

Lomax held the photograph out to her. 'Ever seen this kid?' He studied her eyes intently, then, leaving the photo on her desk, he stood back.

She shook her head. 'Nice looking boy. Rings a bell. But so many of them look the same at that age.' She paused, nervously. 'Why are you looking at me like that?' She shivered, and began to rub her forearms.

'Are you cold?' said Lomax.

'Think I've caught a chill. Got damp in the rain this morning.'

She shuddered, suddenly, then picked the photograph up, and held it out to Lomax. Her hands were shaking, he could see, shaking so much she could hardly hold it. Lomax took it gently from her. 'I've just remembered where I've seen you before. The Manchester Royal Hospital. You were casualty sister, weren't you?'

She looked at him with a slight feeling of relief. 'Yes. Five years ago.'

Lomax nodded. 'Steve had a bad gash – I brought him along for a tetanus jab and stitches.'

She smiled. 'That was before my husband decided to go into the boat business.'

Lomax smiled.

'Thanks for your help,' he said.

Lomax walked out of the marina, turned right, and into the High Street. Nothing much had changed since he had last been up here, except for one old bookshop which had now become part of the Menzies chain, and a trendy vegetarian

28

restaurant that had replaced a rather drab greasy-spoon. He was pleased to note the launderette was still there, checked the closing times on the door, and walked back to his boat. According to Chrissie, Steve had telephoned from somewhere up these parts. According to Spurling, Steve was down in Worcester. He had come up the Trent and Mersey, travelling hard. He would go down the Shropshire Union if he had no joy here, which would give him a wide coverage of the area. If Steve was on the canals, something would lead to him.

He crammed armfuls of sheets, towels and clothes into two plastic bags, then carried them back into the centre of the town.

He filled the washing machine, switched it on, then wandered across the empty launderette, and stared out of the window.

Two teenage boys walked up the street. He looked at them, hope rising suddenly inside him. Equally quickly, it sank again, as they came closer, and neither of them looked remotely like Steve. A green van pulled up, on the other side of the road, but the driver made no attempt to get out. Instinctively, he studied the man, as best he could, through the grubby window of the launderette and the glare off the windscreen of the van. Late twenties; greasy hair; dark glasses. He did not belong. Not here, neither among the locals nor the trippers. A warning bell rang inside him, out of habit. He looked around, again checked the rear exit door of the launderette which he had noted when he had come in. It was habit to him to note all exits. He scanned the street. A couple, in flip flops, husband in khaki shorts, wife in a muslin frock, dragged a bawling child behind them. A young girl stood at a bus stop, wearing a white blouse over her ample bosom. Her boyfriend was pawing amateurishly at her, like a bear trying to break into a honey pot. And then he saw Sally Page, walking up the road, checking her watch, anxious. She overtook several pedestrians, walked past a row of cars, past the green van, and turned left, into an alleyway.

Suddenly, the van driver opened the door, climbed out, and began to walk up the road. Lomax watched him turn off into the same alley as Sally Page. Lomax looked at his watch. Quarter to six. The washing cycle would take another half hour. He walked casually out of the launderette, and crossed the road. He walked as slowly as he dared past the van, peering inside to see what it contained. But it was empty, apart from a petrol can and a coil of rope.

He walked straight past the alleyway, glancing down it in case Sally Page or the driver might be emerging, but there was no sign of them. The alley was narrow and high-walled. It led to some parking bays behind the shops, and then on down to some small warehouses behind the towpath. He returned to the launderette, and memorised the van's licence number.

About twenty minutes later, the van driver returned, walking briskly. He got in the van, and drove off. Keeping his eye on the window, Lomax tugged his laundry out of the machine and crammed it into a spin drier. Forty minutes later, the cycle was finished, and still no sign of her.

'I'm sorry, sir, we're closing now,' said a man in a business suit who had come in, and was removing the cash from the machines.

Lomax scooped up his bags, and walked out into the street. There was a pub across the road. He crossed over, and went in. Two old men were sitting in a window seat playing shove ha'penny, and a blonde sat, with her back to him, on a bar stool, conversing with a couple of elderly trippers.

'I'll have a Carlsberg,' said Lomax, to the barman.

'Did you find the marina?' said a voice beside him.

Lomax turned around; it was the blonde from the barge.

'Yes, thank you.' He looked over at the window.

'On holiday?'

'Yes.' He couldn't talk to her, he had to see what was happening outside.

'Sort of,' he said. 'What about you?'

'Sort of,' she smiled. 'Would you like a drink?'

He held up his half filled glass. 'I'm fine, at the moment,

thank you.'

'I can see that. I asked if you wanted a drink.'

He picked up his glass, awkwardly, and pointed a finger over at a corner table. 'I'll sit over there – for a moment.' He half wanted her to join him, half needed to be alone, to concentrate. 'Would you –?'

'Go ahead,' she said, looking slightly hurt. He had intended her to join him, but she had missed the point. He took his glass, and walked over to the window seat. He put down his laundry bags, and slowly sipped his lager. Still no sign of Sally Page.

The pub filled up, and his laundry bags began to get in the way. Suddenly, he heard a roar outside, and saw the red Porsche, with Sally Page at the wheel, drive past, accelerating hard. He felt relieved and puzzled, at the same time.

He picked up his empty glass and walked back to the bar. But the blonde had gone. 'Damn,' he cursed. He pulled out the photograph of Steve, and handed it to the barman. 'Have you ever seen him?'

The barman took the photo, looked at it for a moment, then shook his head.

'Sorry. No. Looks a bit young to come in here drinking.'

Lomax smiled and nodded. He left the pub, and walked back to his boat.

On board, he cooked a steak, which he had bought in the town that afternoon, opened a bottle of wine, and put a Debussy tape on the stereo. All the time he had been in prison, he had looked forward to getting out, to being free, to getting back to his boat, trying to put the pieces back together. Now he was out, he was back on the boat; it didn't seem so easy any more.

After he had finished supper, he picked up *A Far Sunset*, by Edmund Cooper, and lay down on his wide bunk to see whether life on another planet made any better sense. But he found he kept reading the same page over and over. The same questions came back as had kept coming back in his prison cell. Who? Who? Who? Who had taken the bloody money? One of his workmates? Stratton? Dean? Reynolds? Brabrook? Pember? Pember was the one he trusted the least; but Pember had been the Super's blue-eyed boy. Pember could do no wrong. The sun shone out of his backside, and out of every other bloody orifice. He heard footsteps. On the towpath. Felt a gentle, almost imperceptible sideways movement of the boat; heard another footstep, louder this time. A cold prickle of fear swept through him. He scrabbled his hands around beside him, searching for something heavy, unyielding, that he could use as a weapon. But there was nothing. Another footstep, then another. But there was nothing. He seized his empty wine glass, held it tightly in his clenched fist, ready to smash it into the table, to make it jagged.

The door burst open, swung back on its hinges and banged noisily against the wall.

'Oops – Bugger!' said the blonde girl, standing there with a bemused, slightly tipsy smile, and an unopened bottle of wine in her hand. She peered around in the dim light, until she saw Lomax, and acknowledged him with a wave of her hand. 'Just thought I'd come and say thanks,' she said.

Lomax stared at her in amazement. 'Thanks?'

'Can I come in?'

'Please do.'

She descended the steps, cautiously, then stared nervously at Lomax. 'Your date stand you up?'

Lomax looked up at her and smiled. 'No – I think she just turned up!'

She looked about her, puzzled. 'Where?'

'You,' smiled Lomax.

'Me? Your date?'

'Can't see any other blondes in here.'

She looked at him, studying his face, to see whether he was serious or smiling. She gave a nervous smile. 'I'm not disturbing you, am I?'

'No. Blondes with bottles of wine come wandering in here all the time.' He smiled again, and stood up. 'I'll get you a glass.'

'I'll get one. Tell me where they are.'

He jerked a thumb in the direction of the galley. 'There's some red open, if you'd prefer that?'

'I've been on white tonight – d'you think it's wise to mix them?'

'Live dangerously,' he said.

She came back out of the galley with the glass filled to the brim, sat on the edge of the bunk, sipped the top of the wine, and put the glass down. She leaned forward and gave him a quick peck on the cheek. 'I like you,' she said.

'That's fortunate,' said Lomax.

She giggled. 'You've got a funny way of chatting up women in pubs – wandering off and leaving them.'

'You said you've come to say thanks – what for?' he said.

She smiled. 'I'll tell you in a minute.'

Lomax stared at her smiling face, smelt the pungent perfume; expensive; erotic; no woman had ever smelt so good to him; ever. Somewhere in the last two years, his desire had faded; maybe it was the abstinence; maybe the bromide in the tea. But now, since his release, all his desires had come surging back. He wanted this girl, wanted her more than he had ever wanted any woman in his life.

He grabbed her tightly, pressed his mouth to hers, kissed her passionately, deeply, plunged his tongue into her mouth, fought with her tongue, raced it across her teeth, out of her mouth, around her face, around her ear, inside the ear, around the back of the ear, down the side of her neck, then back, up, back into her mouth, he caressed her face, gently at first, then faster, then pulled her even harder towards him. Suddenly, she jerked away, and took a deep breath.

'Christ!' she said, 'I felt that right down to my heels. When did you last kiss anyone?'

'Give or take a week or so – about two years ago.' He picked up his glass, and took a sip. 'Cheers,' he said, handing her the glass.

'Cheers,' she said, dubiously.

Lomax swung his legs on to the floor, and began to unbutton his shirt.

33

'Hey, hey, whoa, hold a sec.'

'What's the matter?'

'Um – well,' she said. 'I don't even know your name.'

'I don't know yours either, so that's fine. Want a hanger?'

'What are you? The Sebastian Coe of the bedroom? Haven't you heard of the word "woo"?'

'And haven't you heard of the word "prickteaser"?'

She flushed.

'You try to pick me up in the pub, and then you walk into my bedroom holding a bottle of wine. If you don't want to screw, what the hell do you want?'

'I – er –' she looked at him, nervously, her courage gone. 'I poured a gallon of water into my fuel tank instead of diesel.'

Lomax looked at her, stunned. 'So that's why you came to say thanks – in advance!'

She smiled and nodded, then her face went red.

'The smell's different,' he said, helplessly. 'You couldn't confuse them. It's impossible.'

She looked down at the floor. 'I could.'

'So you wanted me to –?'

She nodded, and looked at him. 'Want to throw me out now?'

'No,' he said, leaning forward. 'Later.'

They kissed again, and this time she began to respond, as hard as he. He slipped her tee-shirt up and over her head, ran his hands across her firm breasts, explored her stomach, unbuttoned her jeans, ran his hands over her hips, her thighs, pushed them down inside her underwear, down through the silky hair, felt the cool of the inside of her thighs, the damp, heard the little squeal of delight. It was so long, so long since he had been there, he needed to explore it all, wanted to explore it all. Every part of her body was a treasure trove to him, her toes, the back of her knees, the taut thighs, the cool soft of her buttocks; not only was she a new woman to him, but woman was again new to him, the female body, all new. The last of her clothes slipped away, and he lay between her thighs, his hand slowly gyrating in her dampness, moans from her face that was now twisted against the pillow, now turned up, mouth hungrily open, staring at him. 'Oh yes,' she said. 'Oh yes, oh yes, inside, come inside.'

He stood up, for a moment, on his knees, stared down at the tanned body, with the white breasts and the white band around the thighs. At this moment, he would have done anything for her. He felt like a slave, completely and utterly in her power. He was intoxicated, totally, with her skin, her smell, her softness, her writhing, twisting, snaking flesh. He wanted to make love to her a hundred times tonight, to go on and never stop. Slowly, she pulled him down, guided him to her.

At four in the morning, his strength finally ran out, and he lay back in a river of sweat, completely drained. He heard some early chirping of birds, and the splash of a kingfisher's first strike of the day. He saw the first dull strands of dawn light play across her skin, blurred because it was so close to his eyes.

'I still don't know your name,' she said.

'Lomax. My friends call me Max.'

'Am I your friend?'

'Yes. You're my friend. You haven't told me your name either.'

'Andrea.'

There was a long silence.   'What do you do, Max?'

'Hang around in narrow boats, waiting to get raped. What do you do?'

'I was a housewife, until my husband was killed in a car crash.'

'I'm sorry.'

'Thanks. It was two years ago. I got fed up being a suburban widow.' She paused. 'Actually, I was never particularly happy being a suburban housewife. I'm afraid we didn't have a particularly happy marriage. We did one or two adventure holidays. One was on the canals. I thought I'd come up, and try it again.'

'How long are you here for?'

'A couple more days.'

'How do you find it.'

35

'Different.'

She kissed him lightly on the cheek. 'Goodnight.'

He felt her climb out of the bunk.

'Where you going?' he said.

'Home,' she said. 'Back to my own little boat, like a good little water-rat.'

'You don't have to go,' he said.

'We don't want the neighbours gossiping, do we?'

CHAPTER FIVE

Lomax was panting as he ran across the field that was still damp from dew. He looked at his watch: twenty-five minutes, close on four miles. He turned left at the towpath, ran past Andrea's barge, and stopped at *Harmony*. He reached down and touched his toes.

'Morning, Superman!'

He looked up at the somewhat dishevelled head of Andrea, poking out of her hatch. He blew her a kiss, which she returned.

'What time is it?'

'Nine o'clock.'

'You're up early,' she said.

'Catching worms.'

'Are you going fishing?' she said, missing the joke.

'You could call it that.'

'Want some breakfast first?'

'No thanks. I'm going to have a shower, then I'm off.'

'Am I going to see you again?'

'You promised to cook me dinner tonight. Remember?'

'Just testing!'

Half an hour later, Lomax chugged slowly up towards the Page marina. He saw the red Porsche parked outside the cabin, and steered alongside the fuelling mooring.

As he was about to jump ashore with the stern rope, Sally Page came out of the hut. She looked much brighter, and cheerful.

'I'll take that,' she said. 'Fix the bow line to the far bollard – the other one's worked loose. Did you find your son?'

'No. Not yet. How's the cold?' Lomax took the bow rope, and looped it over the bollard.'

'Better, thanks. What can we do for you?'

'Diesel please.'

She walked to the pump, and pulled the reset lever. She handed Lomax the nozzle, and he took it, unscrewed the fuel tank cap, and pushed in the nozzle. He looked at her. 'Would you come aboard for a second?'

'Aboard?'

He nodded.

She shrugged and stepped onto the boat.

'You're in trouble, aren't you?' he said, gently.

'Me?' she said, surprised. 'Trouble?'

'I've seen the signs too many times, Sally.'

'Have you?' she said, surprise turning to anger.

He nodded. 'You can't get out on your own, you know. Ever. You need help.'

'Just what the hell are you talking about?'

'You know what I'm talking about,' he continued gently, ignoring her rising voice.

'I haven't the foggiest. And it's none of your damned business.'

'I'm afraid it was my damned business. Once you've picked up a few dead, dirty, ruined bodies from shop doorways, derelict warehouses, nice middle-class bedrooms, and once' – his voice began to rise in anger – 'once you've been to the morgue to identify your seven-year-old daughter who's been put there by a heroin-crazed hit and run merchant, it never stops being your business.'

'Are you out of your skull?' she said. 'Fill up your tank and go away.'

'Come on, Sally. You of all people must know the routine, know what has to be done. Godammit, you're a bloody nurse.'

'The name is Mrs Page. Not Sally.'

'All right, Mrs Page. Who's your lover boy in the little green van? Don't tell me a lady of your calibre has it off with pimply greasebugs in alleyways behind towpaths?'

'Have you been following me? What the hell is this? Who the hell are you?'

'My name's Lomax. I'm a friend. That's all.'

'Some friend.'

'And that jerk in the green van – is he a friend? Is he what you'd call a friend? Good friend. Someone you can trust? Is that your type of friend? I know your husband. I've met him a few times. He's a nice man. Dead straight. Successful. Lots of local businesses.'

'All right. How much do you want?'

Lomax stared at her, incredulously. 'For what?'

'For not telling him. He's got heart trouble. If he finds out it'll kill him.'

'I'm not a blackmailer. I don't want money.'

'Then what the hell are you? The good samaritan?'

'Why don't you sit down?'

Still glaring, she perched herself on the deck rail.

'What are you on – horse?'

She shook her head, and her eyes became wet. 'Have you got anything to drink?'

'What would you like?' he asked. 'Tea? Coffee? Something stronger?'

'Tea would be fine.'

'The kettle's still hot. I'll get you some tea. Milk? Sugar?' He pulled the pump out and handed it back to her. Then he went inside. He brought the two teas up, and handed her a mug.

'I'm sorry if I was rude.'

Lomax shrugged and smiled. 'I'm sorry if I'm being personal.' He paused, and stared gently at her. 'How? How did it happen?'

'Couple of years ago I had an accident, skiing. It wasn't set properly – French quack. I had a hell of a lot of pain, and I dulled it with drugs I used to get from the hospital.'

'Get?' said Lomax.

She grinned, and then flushed. 'Took. Pinched. Not difficult.'

'Methadene.'

39

She looked at him, surprised. 'You know your drugs – what are you – drugs squad, or something?'

Lomax smiled. 'The irony is that methadene is used in the clinics to help addicts unhook.'

'Dependents,' said Sally, emphatically. 'Not addicts.'

Lomax smiled again, gently.

'Leslie's heart trouble started – had a couple of bad attacks: someone had to be home with him day and night. I wasn't going to let anyone else do it, so I left the hospital.'

'And lost your supply?' So you turned to horse?'

She nodded, and swallowed hard.

'Sniffing or smoking?'

'Injecting.'

Lomax looked at her, surprised. 'That serious? How much?'

'A quarter of a grain.'

'A day?'

'Yes.'

'I'm surprised your friend in the green van doesn't drive a Rolls Royce.'

'I expect he will do soon, the way he keeps upping the price.'

'Name of the game,' said Lomax. 'Once a pusher's got his mark hooked –' he jerked his thumb upwards.'And you've got no other source?'

She shook her head.

'Street price has halved in the last year.'

'So I've read. How much should a gramme cost today?'

'Sixty quid – seventy quid. No more.'

'I pay double that.'

'Unfortunately,' said Lomax, 'pushers don't advertise in the Yellow Pages.' He took a sip of his tea. 'You must be getting through a bit of the old housekeeping.'

'I don't think I can keep it from my husband much longer. I've been selling my jewellery; my clothes; premium bonds.' She began to cry. 'I'm frightened,' she said. 'God, I'm so frightened.'

A car drove into the marina, and parked. Lomax watched

a man get out, and walk into the office. A moment later, he came out, looked around, then began to walk down towards them.

'You've got a punter coming,' said Lomax. 'When's your next purchase?'

'Lunchtime today. Bastard put the price up again yesterday. I only had enough for one hit.'

'Have you got any wheels I could borrow?'

She jerked her thumb over her shoulder. 'Take the Porsche.'

'Something not quite as conspicuous?'

'We've got a little van – runabout.'

'Anything painted on it? Name?'

She shook her head. 'No.'

'Perfect,' he said.

CHAPTER SIX

It began to rain; heavy, sheeting summer rain. The din inside the van was almost deafening as for a moment the rain turned to hail, then back to rain again. Lomax sat patiently, watching the road through the windscreen. Every few minutes he switched the wipers on for one wipe. Conditions could not have been better.

A heavy lorry thundered past, shaking the small van, and then another. He saw a blur of red, and gave the wipers one wipe. It was the Porsche. It waited at the junction between the track and the road, then pulled out, turned right, and accelerated off past him on the opposite side of the road. Lomax saw the slight movement of her head, the merest hint of an acknowledgement, and smiled grimly.

A couple of minutes later, the green van appeared. It stopped at the junction for a brief moment, then turned left. Lomax started the engine, saw another lorry coming up in his mirror, let it pass, then pulled out behind it.

The lorry and the green van travelled at the same speed for a couple of miles, then Lomax saw the lorry's left indicator and brake lights come on. In front of it, he saw the green van turn left. Lomax looked at the signposts. The road would take them down to the canal – the lorry would be going down to one of the wharves.

They drove past a cement works, and then came to a massive timber yard fronting the canal. The lorry turned right, into the yard. Lomax watched the green van turn left, along the road behind the towpath. There was a *Dead End* warning sign on it. Lomax turned sharply right, and pulled up behind a pile of logs and a cabin cruiser on a cradle. He got out of the car and began to run, in the driving rain, up the dead-end road. After about three hundred yards he rounded a corner and saw the van, in the car park of what looked like a derelict pub. The forlorn sign 'Number One' was still attached to the wall, and most of the windows were boarded up. Lomax pushed into a sodden hedge, and stood, watching. He glanced at his watch, wondering how long he would have to wait, and hoping this was the right place.

After less than a couple of minutes, the pusher came round from the side of the pub, got in the van and drove off. Lomax waited until he heard him accelerate off on the main road, and then walked up to the pub. All the downstairs doors were barred up. The building had a ghostly, eerie feel to it. He walked right around the building, wondering how the pusher had got in. Then he saw the rusting fire escape scaling the side. He ran up it, and pushed open the door at the top. It opened without resistance, and he found himself in an upstairs dance floor, with a bar at one end. The place obviously hadn't been used in years, and apart from one broken chair, covered in dust, there was no furniture. He walked across the floor to the far window and looked out. The canal was right in front, and he watched a coaler sliding slowly past.

He searched the upstairs carefully, then saw a set of wet footprints at the top of the internal staircase. He went down, conscious of the sound of dripping water everywhere, and of a strange clacking sound that he found unnerving: like a cupboard door banging in the wind, except there was no wind.

He went down into the lavatories. The clacking sound came from one of the cubicles. He pushed open the door sharply, and stood to one side. Water was brimming over the top of the lavatory cistern, in steady surges. Each surge lifted the lid, and as the water released, the lid banged down. He walked through the puddle of water that was rapidly spreading across the floor, and stood on the seat. He pushed back his sleeve, lifted the lid, and put his hand inside. He pulled out a thick oilskin package. He replaced the lid, and walked up the stairs again to the saloon bar. He laid the package on top of the counter. It was folded over several times, and then zipped. Inside was another packet. He opened that too, and tipped six smaller packages onto the counter.

He opened one: it was full of white tablets. He tipped them out, carefully, onto the counter. He didn't need a chemist to tell him what they were.

Suddenly, he heard an engine – a vehicle travelling fast. Then it slowed, there was the sound of tyres on gravel, and the ratchet of a hand brake. He stayed motionless at the counter while footsteps on the fire escape echoed around the room. The upstairs door banged open, banged shut.

Frantically, Lomax stuffed everything into his jacket pockets, slid himself over the counter, and crouched down behind it. He picked up a dusty Stout bottle, gripping it firmly by the neck. Someone hurried across the floor, through another door, and then footsteps clumped down the internal staircase. He heard a couple of loud sniffs, then someone walked across the floor, through another door – to the lavatories, he thought, as the footsteps faded down the basement steps.

Silently, clutching the bottle tightly, he heaved himself back over the bar, and ran equally silently to the basement door. He heard footsteps, hurrying this time, up the stone stairs, and he flattened himself against the wall, raising the bottle. But the steps stopped. There was a long silence. Then he heard a click: the dull menacing click of a flick-knife. He knew the sound well – the standard weapon of the street pusher.

Suddenly, and quite unexpectedly, the door cracked open, and the man twisted through, like a snake. Lomax cracked the bottle down, but missed the man's head and caught him a glancing blow on the shoulder – the wrong shoulder. The man rolled over, and was on his feet, crouched, in a fighting position, still holding the knife. The man was Sally's pusher.

'Who the hell are you?' he said.

'I just popped by for a drink,' said Lomax.

'Let's have it back,' said the pusher, holding his knife forward.

Lomax replied by smashing the bottom of the bottle off against the wall, and holding forward the jagged neck he jumped sideways, landing on the balls of his feet – then tipped forward, on to his toes.

The pusher lunged at him, and Lomax ducked sideways, kicking the man's feet away. Before the man hit the ground, Lomax smashed a karate chop on to his arm, sending the knife scudding across the floor, grabbed the hair at the back of his head, and banged his forehead onto the floor, once, hard, then again, harder. The pusher keeled over, dazed, then Lomax slammed a rabbit punch into the nape of his neck, knocking him out cold.

Working quickly, he whipped the pusher's belt out of his trousers, and strapped his hands tightly together behind his back. He then pulled down the man's trousers, and bound his legs together tightly with them. Then he dragged him over to the wall, and sat him, half upright, leaning against it. Then he began to slap the man's face, gently at first, then harder to bring him round.

Slowly, the man's eyes opened, and he began to look around. He glared at Lomax, in a mixture of hatred and fear.

Lomax slowly and deliberately walked over to the flick-knife and picked it up. He knelt down in front of the pusher, dug his left hand into his pocket, and pulled out a handful of heroin tablets. Then, holding the razor sharp knife in his right hand, he brought the blade close to the man's face. The man squirmed.

'I wouldn't wriggle if I were you, my friend. Could do yourself a nasty accident.'

The pusher, trembled. Lomax held the handful of pills up to the pusher's mouth. 'Hungry?' he said.

The man's eyes filled with terror. 'No,' he said. 'No.'

'Open wide, and say "aaah".'

'No. Please no. I'll give you the money.'

'Thank you. I've already got the money. Open wide.'

'It'll kill me.'

'Well done. You're catching on fast.'

'No. Please no.'

'You're a lucky fellow. Did you know that? Today's your lucky day. You've actually got a choice. You eat these tablets, or you get cut. Which would you like?' Lomax pressed the knife closer.

'No! Please no!'

As the man screamed out, Lomax rammed his fist into his mouth, wrenching it open. He released the pills, then slammed his fist into the man's stomach. The man gasped, and began to choke.

'Don't be a greedy boy. Shouldn't take such big mouthfuls.' Lomax slammed his fist again into his stomach. The man's mouth flew open and his head crashed back against the wall, as he gulped for air.

Lomax walked over to the bar counter, picked up a filthy glass and filled it from the cold tap; he walked back over to the pusher and poured the water into his mouth; the pusher spluttered it down. Lomax put down the glass and looked inside his mouth, carefully. 'Good boy,' said Lomax. 'All gone.'

He tugged the packets of tablets out of his pockets, and stuffed them into the pusher's pockets. Carefully, he turned his own pockets inside out, shaking out the loose pills that remained. Then he knelt down and looked at the pusher's eyes. The fear was already turning into a glazed stupefied look.

Lomax stood up. 'Want to come for a walk?'

The eyes rolled up at him, had difficulty in focusing, and rolled away again.

Lomax untied him, pulled his trousers back up, put the belt back around his waist. 'Sweet dreams,' he said, turning and walking out.

Three miles down the road, Lomax spotted a call box. He went in, and dialled 999.

'Police,' he said, when it was answered.

'There's a derelict pub near the canal – Number One. Know it?'

'Yes.'

'There's a man in there with a bad headache. Think he's overdosed on heroin. You'll need an ambulance, and you'd better hurry.' He hung up, left the booth, and drove off.

Lomax waited outside the office at the Page marina, whilst Sally served a customer. The rain had stopped and the afternoon sun felt warming. The customer left, and Lomax walked in.

'Hello,' she said, nervously. 'How did you get on?'

'Laugh a minute. Got a piece of paper?'

She handed him a notebook. He picked a pencil off the desk, and scrawled on the paper. Then he tore off the sheet and handed it back to her. 'Best in the country. Private. Run by three wise monkeys. Hear no evil, see no evil, speak no evil. They'll get anyone off the hook. Even you.'

'Is it private?'

'Very private.'

'It'll cost a bomb.' She raised her hands. 'Where can I get that sort of money?'

'Try your local friendly magician. Now you don't see it, now you do.' He dug his hand into his breast pocket and pulled out an oilskin package. He put it down on the desk. 'Three grand, give or take a pound.'

'Yours?'

'No. Yours – and others. As we can hardly advertise for the rest of its rightful owners, it might as well go towards one good charity. You.'

'What do I tell Leslie?'

'Tell him you're going to a health farm.'

'He needs me.'

'If he needs you, then all the more reason to do it. You won't be much use to him when you're dead – from an overdose, or from a rusty needle, or the wrong damned chemical, or any of the other damned things that kill junkies every day of the week – decent people, Sally. People who have a right to wake up in the morning without having to worry where the next fix's coming from. Decent people, who deserve to go through life without having to sit on lavatory floors, strapping cords around their arms and legs to pop out their veins.' He looked at her, kindly.

'How do you know I won't just find another pusher, and carry on.'

Lomax shrugged. 'I don't. The choice is yours.' He turned, and walked out the door.

'Hey!' She called. 'Hey!'

He turned.

She was smiling at him. 'Thanks,' she said.

'You're welcome.'

CHAPTER SEVEN

Lomax leaned back on his seat, and stretched out. Then he leaned forward, raised his wine glass, and chinked glasses with Andrea. He smiled at her across the candlelit table. 'Cheers,' he said. 'Thank you for a fantastic meal.'

Andrea smiled. 'Thank you for draining my tank.'

'You thanked me last night; and the night before; and the night before that.'

'What about the night before that? Did I forget that one?'

'No – I'm sure you didn't.'

They chinked glasses again. Lomax suddenly reached under his seat, and pulled out a small gift-wrapped package. He blushed, and handed it to her. 'For you. I bought you a little present.'

She took it, surprised. 'A present? Me?'

He nodded at her, smiling.

'Thank you – but why?'

'Because I like you. You've been good to me. Good for me. It's to say thank you for being a very lovely person.'

It was her turn to flush. She opened the package carefully, and pulled out a huge silk scarf. 'Wow,' she said, holding it up, first to the candle-light, and then pressing it against her skin. 'That's beautiful, Max. She looked at it closely. 'Cornelia James! my favourite scarves... my absolute favourite. Max, you shouldn't have, you really shouldn't have.'

He grinned. 'Well, I did.'

She leaned forward and kissed him gently on the forehead. Then she kissed him on the mouth: a long, lingering kiss.

'Thank you,' she said. 'I'm glad you did.'

He smiled at her. 'I don't want you to go tomorrow.'

'I could only extend the barge hire because they had a cancellation – it's fully booked for the season. I have to hand it back tomorrow. Anyway, if I hire it much longer, I might as well buy it!'

'Why not? Why don't you?' he said, seriously.

Andrea laughed.

'You could stay here. A few days,' said Lomax. 'Travel with me. There are some incredibly beautiful things to see.'

She shrugged her shoulders. 'I suppose I could stay on for a few days,' she said, and her eyes lit up. Her expression touched Lomax: there seemed to be such sadness in that pretty face, and now, for a moment, the sadness was gone, and it was happy.

As they lay in bed, Lomax heard a motorcycle engine roar into life: it seemed only a short distance away.

'You don't talk about yourself, do you?' said Andrea, gently stroking his chest. 'Tell me about you.'

Lomax traced a line around her navel. 'Not much to tell.'

'I don't believe that,' she said, laughingly.

'True.'

'Are you married?'

'No.'

'Never?'

'Once.'

'Any children?'

'Once.'

'I'm sorry.'

'Don't be.'

There was a long pause. He could still hear the motorcycle, in the distance, receding into the night.

'Do you live here all the time? Is this your home?'

'Yes.'

'Do you like living on a barge?'

'Narrow-boat,' he chided, gently. 'They're called narrow-boats.' He paused, and would have liked a cigarette now; but

50

he had quit, and had stayed quit for eighteen months, and was determined to remain quit. 'Living on a narrow-boat's a bit like being a snail. Go everywhere with one's home on one's back. I don't like being cooped up, shut in.'

'Don't you call this being cooped up?'

'No, I'm free. I like it. I like not having a telephone; not having to pay the rates. I like not having a postal code. I don't have to worry every Friday how big the milk bill's going to be. I like not having a front door for the Watchtower people to knock on. Yes. I like it.'

She kissed him gently on the chest. 'I can understand that,' she said. 'Quite a difference to suburbia.' There was a silence for a moment. 'And do you work – or are you an eccentric millionaire?'

'I work, from time to time, when I need money. There's always jobs going around the canals. Casual jobs.'

'The modern-day Sir Galahad. Charging around the waterways on your shining steed; dashing to the rescue of damsels in distress; rescuing them from the perils of water in their diesel tanks.'

'You got it,' said Lomax.

She laughed, then rolled on top of him. 'How's your lance?' she said.

The following morning, they cruised in convoy up the canal. The sky was clear blue, and Lomax peeled off his tee-shirt, and sat at the tiller in jeans and bare feet. He turned and gave a cheery wave at the helmswoman behind him, in his wake. Andrea waved back.

The canal widened as they came to the fork with the River Dee, outside Chester, then narrowed again.

Lomax heard a motorcycle engine. It was the second time he had been aware of one this morning. Earlier, it had been the gentle throb, of a rider cruising. Now, suddenly, it was a short roar, the sound of a bike accelerating hard.

He looked beyond the fields to his left, at the road. A large delivery van overtook a couple of cyclists, and a squad of boy scouts. But no sign of any motorcycle.

When they reached Ross Harcourt's boatyard, he jumped on to the pontoon and secured *Harmony* on one of the visitor's moorings. Then he guided Andrea on to the hire-boat mooring.

The ramrod-straight figure of Ross Harcourt appeared, moustache as close-trimmed as a privet hedge, cavalry twills immaculately creased, brogues spit-and-polished. 'Morning Lomax, haven't seen you in a while,' he barked, in his clipped, unwelcoming, military voice.

Lomax did not like the man, but respected the immaculate way in which he ran his business and kept his boats. In a neck of the woods already noted for its peace and quiet, the safest peace and quiet of all was to be found in the sanctuary of his moorings. For those that wanted to discover the call of the wild, but under the dutiful eye of a headmaster, there was no better place than Harcourt's Nature Marina.

'Haven't been up this way for a while, Colonel,' said Lomax. 'Been down Worcester way.'

'Not what I read.'

Harcourt looked at Lomax with his usual deadpan expression. It was impossible to tell whether it was meant to convey sympathy or disdain; but Lomax strongly suspected it was the latter. 'Man of your calibre, Colonel, shouldn't be reading the tabloids.'

Harcourt grunted. 'Anyhow, what brings you here? Want to use the phone or borrow a hammer?'

'I'm doing you a favour for a change, Colonel.'

'It is Brigadier, actually,' he said patiently.

'Sorry,' said Lomax. 'I'm not very good with army terminology – being a seafarer.'

'Seafarer!' snorted Ross. 'Bloody water-gypsy, I'd say. What's this favour?'

Lomax jerked his thumb over his shoulder. 'One of your punters – delivering her safely back.'

'Doesn't look as if she needs any help to me.'

'She did last week. Filled her diesel tank with water; other side of Lymm.'

Harcourt grunted a grudging thanks. 'How much are you

going to charge me for that?'

'Come on, Gen – er – Brigadier, give me some credit – I'm not all bad. There's no charge. Maybe I'll need a favour from you one day.'

Harcourt grunted again. Lomax pulled out the photograph, and handed it to him. 'By the way – you haven't seen him lately, have you?'

'Your boy, isn't it?' said Harcourt. 'Seen him with you in the past. Run away, has he?'

Lomax nodded.

Harcourt shook his head. 'I'll keep my eye out. What do you want me to do if I see him?'

'Ask him to call Jack Spurling. Spurling's Yard – Grand Union – Leighton Buzzard.' Lomax paused. 'Actually, that reminds me, maybe I will make a call.'

'Using up your favour?' This time there was a distinct grin on the old soldier's face.

'Come off it,' said Lomax. 'It took me three hours to clean that sodding tank. Would have cost you a lot of bread to have had someone do it for you – and you'd never have got the boat back today.'

Harcourt nodded, grudgingly, again. 'In the office.'

Jack Spurling had one message for him. His mother was ill: would he please contact his sister urgently.

Lomax came out of the office with a grim face. He waited outside whilst Andrea and Harcourt went in to settle her bill, then took her suitcase and dumped it on board *Harmony*.

After five minutes, she joined him, and gave him a big kiss on the cheek. 'Aren't you going to pipe me aboard?' she said.

He smiled at her. It took an effort.

'What's up?' she said. 'Have you changed your mind?'

'No. No. Nothing like that. Let's move on, shall we? This place always depresses me. You're in charge of for'ard ropes from now on – I believe in making my crew work.' He grinned again, a warmer grin this time.

'Aye, aye, captain.'

They tied up to a couple of trees, and had a picnic lunch in the woods beside the canal. 'I'm beginning to see the attractions,' she said, lying back and staring at the sunlight through the leaves. 'I didn't particularly enjoy the week on my own. Certainly making up for it now. What's it like in winter?'

'Cold. Wet. Damp. Lonely.'

'How do you keep warm?'

'Got central heating on the boat.'

'Central heating? You're kidding. I suppose you're going to tell me you've got double glazing as well?'

'Thinking about it,' he said, absently.

'Hey – what's the matter – have I upset you?'

'No. Had a bit of bad news this morning – I made a call from Harcourt's office. My mother's ill. A stroke.'

'Oh. I'm sorry. Where is she?'

'London. Hendon. I'm going to have to pop down there.'

'A bad stroke?'

'Don't know. They won't know for a few days. She had one before.' He paused for a long moment, and looked down at the ground. 'Two years ago.'

'Are you very close?'

'We were. Once. But my father and I haven't seen eye to eye –' he paused again '– lately. So I haven't been there for a long time. I ought to go now – you know – in case.'

She suddenly felt cold and shivered. She looked up at the sky, but no cloud had come over. 'I might as well travel down with you, then. I'm going the same direction.'

'No,' he said. 'Don't go. Not just yet. I only want to pop down there, just see her, just have a few hours with her. If I leave this afternoon, I could be back tomorrow afternoon.' He paused and looked at her. 'Would you stay?'

She smiled. 'If you'd like me to.'

'I would.' He looked at his watch, and listened to the sound of the wood. Somewhere he heard a branch snapping. Was it his imagination? An animal? Or? He'd heard a motorbike again this morning. Maybe he was getting paranoid. Lots of people on the canals had motorbikes, kept them on their barges. 'Yes, I could easily get there by this evening. I think we'll moor in Harcourt's marina; you'll be safe there.'

'Safe?' she said, incredulously.

He cursed himself for the slip of the tongue. 'Get a lot of vandals, petty thieves on the canals – like anywhere. Better to have other boats around you.'

'But I've been sleeping out all week on my own,' she said. 'I thought that was the point. Getting away from it all.'

Lomax smiled. 'This is a lot bigger boat than the one you hired. Do you really want to handle it on your own?'

She looked down towards the water and shook her head. 'No.'

'Harcourt owes me a favour,' he said. 'I'm sure he'll be delighted to loan us the bridal mooring.'

'How will you travel?'

'Hitch.'

'You'll call me, won't you,' she said, 'If you're not going to be back tomorrow?'

'Yes. But I'll be back. And I don't want you picking up any strange bargees in pubs. People who mess around in boats are a weird lot.'

'So I've noticed,' she said, giving him a playful punch.

CHAPTER EIGHT

The lorry dropped Lomax on the Edgware Road, at eight o'clock in the evening. He took the tube the rest of the way, and walked up to the front door of his sister and brother-in-law's small terraced house, half an hour later.

His sister greeted him the way she had always greeted him: like a stranger towards whom she had a duty to be tolerant and helpful. Lomax followed her through into the living room which always made him wince in horror. Every inch of shelf was covered in china knick-knacks, ranging from flamenco dancers with serene imbecilic faces, to french poodles with bows in their hair. Every inch of floor was covered in half-eaten toys, and evey inch of furniture in doilies.

'Where's Geoff?' he asked.

'Out. His snooker night.'

'How're the kids?'

'Tiring.'

He looked at her pale, tired middle-aged face. She had always been middle-aged. She had been born middle-aged.

'Would you like a drink?'

'What have you got?'

She opened a cupboard and looked in. 'Sweet sherry?' she suggested, hopefully.

'Or?'

'There's some green stuff we brought back from Greece. Not very nice – and it's a few years old.'

'No thanks,' said Lomax. 'How about a coffee?'

'I'll go and make you one.'

'Thanks. So how is Mum?'

'Not good. Just sits. Doesn't respond to anything?'

'Which hospital's she in?'

Karen stared at him. 'She's not – she's back at home. It was three weeks ago.'

'Why the hell didn't you tell me then?'

She shrugged. 'Dad didn't want me to. Didn't want anyone to. Said you'd only upset her.'

'Might upset him,' said Lomax, bitterly. 'But not her. He might want to disown me; she still feels some spark for me.' He paused, and picked up a china goblin.

'I'm sorry I didn't call you sooner, Max. I – well, in any case, I thought they wouldn't have let you out, so you'd only have worried. I'll make your coffee.'

She went out of the room. Lomax picked up the telephone and dialled.

'Lomax here,' said a gruff voice.

'Hallo, Dad.'

The voice went cold. 'Yes?'

'It's Max.'

'Yes?'

'I'd like to come and see mother.'

'What do you want to do? Kill the poor woman off? She's suffered enough by you. Can't you leave her in peace? Haven't you done enough?'

'Have you asked her?' said Lomax, bitterness rising in his voice. 'Have you bloody asked her?'

'I'll not have you swearing at me down this phone.'

'Look – I'm at Karen's. I could be there in half an hour. Just give me five mintues with her. That's all.' He heard a firm click, and found he was talking into a silent receiver. He hung up, and stood, head bowed. Slowly, he shook his head. He stayed there for several minutes.

'Dad?'

He turned round. Karen was standing there with a tray. He nodded.

'Reckons your being convicted was what gave her her first stroke.'

He took a cup and a couple of digestive biscuits and sat down, clearing a fire engine out of the way with his feet.

'He talks about you as though you were the Yorkshire Ripper.'

'I was set up. Stitched up. Can't he bloody believe his own son?'

'Not many people have believed you so far.' From her tone, he knew she didn't either.

'You don't have to remind me. I lost my job, my career, two years of my life, my wife, my son, my home. Now I'm not even allowed to visit my mother when she's sick. She may be on her deathbed – and I don't even get the bloody chance to tell her my side, so she can decide for herself.'

Karen looked at him sadly, and spoke for a moment with genuine sympathy. 'I'm sorry for you. I think you ought to be allowed to see her. I think that, whatever else.' She stirred her coffee. 'Any sign of Steve?'

'No. He's on the canals somewhere, I'm sure. People have seen him.' He bit savagely into a biscuit.

'Don't be bitter with Dad,' she said. 'You know what he's like.'

'Oh, sure,' he said, venomously.

'Look, Max, you were never his kind of policeman. "Cut glass coppers", you know his phrase. King's Road suits. Curzon Street haircuts. Fancy music.'

Lomax laughed, bitterly. 'Because I don't like John Phillip Souza?'

'Not that – not just that. Hundreds of little things, all add up. You prefer wine to beer –'

'Only with bloody food!' he exploded.

'You've mixed with some strange types,' she went on, ignoring his outburst. 'Dope freaks, acid heads...'

'But that's the point,' he said, exasperated. 'You can't work the drugs scene looking like Dixon of Dock Green! He doesn't understand, or want to understand. Things have changed, even in the Force.'

Karen smiled. 'He was on about "Real Bobbying" the other day. Talks about it like it was Real Ale. Words you never hear any more. A good old Ding Dong. A ramsammy. All the world's problems could be solved by a size twelve up the backside.' She smiled, and sipped her coffee again. 'You have to try to understand how he feels. Twenty-eight years in the force. You come in, his pride and joy.'

'I was never his pride and joy.'

'You were, Max. More than you ever realised. He was able to say to his mates: "That's my boy – Lomax, P.C. Lomax. Fulham, he's at now." Then you and the drugs squad mob became a law of your own. He was horrified.'

'That's ridiculous. We never did.'

'It looked that way to him. Grubby clothes, jeans, long hair, flash suits. How do you think he felt? To have his mates ribbing him; and all the time have to defend you, and stick up for you. And then, suddenly, all the jokes and all the ribbing have a horrible ring of truth: you're arrested and convicted – his son. He gets anonymous calls in the middle of the night – even now they go on – asking him where he got the money for his new car.' She looked at him sadly, picked up a pack of Stuyvesant and offered them to him.

'No thanks, I quit.'

'So it did you some good, then, being inside?'

'Oh yes,' he said. 'It did me some good.'

CHAPTER NINE

At half past eight, the midges became too much for her. Exasperated, Andrea smacked at her forearm, and missed again. She stood up, and began to clear away her supper things from the open cockpit of *Harmony*. It was a balmy warm evening, and she wished that Lomax would suddenly reappear.

She went below and wondered whether to read for a while, but she wasn't in the mood for reading. She changed into a smart blouse, put on a splash of make-up and her new scarf, and went ashore.

As she walked out of the marina gates, she scarely noticed a blue motorcycle propped against one of the alleyway walls opposite.

She walked past one pub, which seemed very quiet, and went into another, where a sing-song was in progress. She sipped her way slowly through a couple of gin and tonics, and successfully resisted the invitations to a party, that were thrust at her at regular intervals from a trio of drunken handbag sales reps.

She made her escape shortly before closing time, whilst the three reps were ensuring that they would have a supply of full glasses when the gong went. She walked slowly through the warm darkness towards the marina. She passed the alleyway, where the motorcycle was still parked, and went in through the well-lit entrance to the marina.

She walked around the bank, cutting across the wet grass, and trying to be careful not to trip over any ropes. There were several boats of similar size parked together, and it took her a moment to work out which one was *Harmony*. As she approached it, she checked the name on the stern, to be sure, then went aboard. She unlocked the cabin door, and decided to leave it ajar to let some air into the stuffy interior. She switched the saloon light on, walked down the steps and over to the budgerigar cage. The bird was sitting on its perch, with its head resting on its wing.

'Goodnight, Frankie,' she said, smiling at it. 'I won't forget your breakfast in the morning. Tell me whether you'd like bacon and eggs or a kipper?' She waited for a moment, then shrugged. 'Haven't made your mind up yet? All right – fill in the form and leave it on the back of your cage door.'

A strange tearing sound awoke her, and the sudden flare of a bright light. The light subsided and became a red glow: she smelt the sweet smoke of a cigarette.

'Max? Is that you?' she said, puzzled.

The red glowed brighter for a second.

'Max?'

Something wasn't right and she couldn't work out what. Then a spasm of fear shook her. Max didn't smoke, she remembered. 'Who's that?' she said, whispering. There was no response. 'Who is that?' She felt something crawl up the back of her neck, and she smacked wildly at it; but it was nothing. 'Who is that?' She tried to shout, but it came out only as a strangled squeak. She scrabbled with her arm for the light switch, trying desperately to remember where it was. Something crashed to the floor. A book. 'Who is that?' Her glass of water crashed to the floor. 'Who are you? Please, who are you? Max, is that you? How's your mother, Max?' she said, pleading now, pleading that it would be Max. She found the switch, pressed it, and for a moment she was blinded by the light. She screwed her eyes up, and then opened them, slowly. A man in leather motorcycling gear was sitting calmly in the chair beside the bed, smoking a cigarette. He smiled gently at her. Max has had an accident, she thought.

He took another long drag of the cigarette, in no hurry to

speak, and smiled at her. This time it was more of a leer. It was a small, weasely face, greasy from sweat, with short, limp hair, crudely cut. Two of his front teeth were missing.

'Who – who are you?' she said. 'What do you want?'

'You smell anything?' He spoke with a smug, patronising voice.

'I beg your pardon?'

'Smell. Can you smell anything?'

She sniffed hard. 'Smoke?'

'Clever. Anything else?'

'Yes – there is something else – what is it?'

'Why don't you try to guess, lady? Women are meant to be smart these days.'

The man frightened her. She wanted to give him the answer, give him the right answer. Maybe, she thought, irrationally, if she gave him the right answer he would go away. She sniffed hard. The smell didn't make sense; she began to recognise it, but still it didn't make sense.

'It smells a bit like petrol.'

'Now you're getting the hang of things. Do you know why it smells like petrol?'

'No. Why?'

'Because it is petrol.' He gave a broad grin, and held up a yellow tin of Ronson lighter fluid. Then he put it in his pocket, and trod his cigarette out on the floor.

'Hey!' she said, angry for a brief moment. She wanted to shout at him, tell him off, but as suddenly as her anger had come it went, replaced again by fear.

'Worried I might burn the floor? Would be a shame, wouldn't it?' He put another cigarette in his mouth, and held up the box of matches in his hand. He shook it, slowly, unhurriedly, as the cigarette dangled from his lips.

Andrea stared at him, wide eyed, and began to shake with terror. 'Petrol?' she said. 'I don't understand.'

'Feel your blankets,' he said.

Slowly, she reached out her hand, and touched the top of the bedclothes. She recoiled with revulsion. 'Ugh, they're wet.'

'That's right,' he said. 'They're wet.'

'Why?'

Slowly, he shook the matchbox in front of her; just enough so that the matches rattled together.

Andrea looked down at the wet bedclothes that were pulled up to her chest, and at the matches. The man was mad, she knew, a nutter. Humour him: try to humour him. How? 'Who are you?' she asked, as brightly as she could. 'Are you a friend of Max's?'

Naylor began to laugh, a few chortles. 'That's good,' he said. 'I like it.'

She smiled too, trying to encourage him; but the humour suddenly vanished from his face, like a slide change on a projection screen. 'I ask the questions,' he said, angrily. 'Not you. Where is he? Mr One Hundred Percent.'

'I'm sorry; I don't understand.'

He rattled the box of matches again.

'Do you mean Max?'

'Who do you think I mean, sweetheart? The Pope?'

'London. Gone to London.'

'To buy some sparklers?'

'To see his mother. She's ill. Had a stroke.'

'I'm sorry – send her my condolences. When's he due back?'

'I don't know,' she said, suddenly afraid of saying too much, of putting Lomax in danger.

The man rolled the cigarette across his lips with his tongue. 'How about the money, then? We can have a little chat about it. Yeah, better without him. Know what I mean?'

'I'm – er –'

'Where does he keep it?'

'What money?'

'You were doing quite well a moment ago, sweetheart. Don't go stupid on me.'

'I don't think he has much money.'

'Not what I've heard.' He shook the matchbox again, menacingly. 'What's your name?'

She stared blankly at him for a moment, terror seizing her

again. He rattled the matchbox.

'Andrea.'

'Nice name. Pretty. Pretty face you got too. 'Spect you know that – don't need me to tell you that.' He rolled the unlit cigarette back across his lips. 'You ever seen anyone with multiple burns?'

She shook her head.

'Not pretty,' he said, shaking the matchbox again. 'The money. What's he done with it?'

'I don't know. I really don't know. I don't know him, hardly at all... We only met a short while ago, for Chrissake.'

'And now you're shacking up with him. One of you's a fast worker. Might ask you for advice on technique one day. Seen him go to a bank?'

'No.'

'You sound frightened.'

His voice was suddenly friendlier. She relaxed, a fraction, and tried to smile. 'I am frightened.'

The man looked at her and smiled kindly. 'Long as you tell the truth,' he said, 'there's no need to be frightened.' He struck a match and lit the cigarette. He inhaled deeply, took another long drag, and inhaled that too. 'Bad habit, smoking,' he said. 'Must quit one day.' He looked up at her. 'Perhaps you'd like a little souvenir of our chat; something you can show to Lomax when he returns – know what I mean?'

'Yes,' she said, uncertainly. 'Of course.'

'Good.' He took another deep drag on the cigarette, then tossed it onto the centre of the bed.

CHAPTER TEN

Lomax was tired when he arrived back at the Harcourt marina, shortly after noon, the following day. He had spent a sleepless night on the sofa of his sister's house. The bitterness of his father had burned in his mind, making sleep impossible.

At five o'clock in the morning he had left the house, and had waited nearly three hours at the start of the M1 before a truck stopped for him. There seemed to be an unusual amount of activity in the marina: boats which would normally have been out on the canal at this time were still moored, and their occupants were on deck, looking at him strangely. He walked up to *Harmony*, and saw Frankie hanging outside, in his cage. Perhaps Andrea was spring cleaning, he thought. He smelt the pungent smell of burned wood, and burned plastic. Someone had had a bonfire, he thought.

'Christ!' he said, as he got closer to the boat, and saw that the bank beside it was littered with charred debris.

He jumped aboard. 'Andrea!' He shouted, anxiously. 'Andrea?'

The stench was overpowering as he went through into the saloon; but there was no sign of any fire, apart from an empty extinguisher lying on the floor. He walked through into the bedroom, and recoiled in horror. The bunk was completely burned out. The bedclothes, with black holes, were strewn on the floor in puddles of water. The curtains were tattered, with jagged black sections at the bottom, and the walls and the ceiling were covered in what looked like black treacle. Everywhere, there were great splodges of white foam. He ran back out onto the deck. An elderly couple were sitting in their cockpit eating lunch in the barge in the next mooring.

'What happened?' he shouted. 'What happened?'

The old man looked up, chewing a mouthful slowly; then he looked down, and began to cut himself a piece of ham.

'What happened?' Lomax said, louder.

The woman gave him a strange look, then helped herself to some more wine. 'I think there was a fire,' she said, in a thick Lancashire accent.

'Think?' he said, incredulously. 'You think there was a fire?'

'Aye,' said the man, still chewing. 'Aye, there was a fire.' He looked back down at his food.

'Was anyone on board?'

The man shrugged, and carefully sawed a radish in half.

'Not very curious, are you?' shouted Lomax. He jumped off the barge, and stormed across to Harcourt's office.

Harcourt was seated at his desk, totting up a row of figures with an immaculate yellow pencil; he didn't glance up until he had got to the bottom.

'What the hell's happened to my boat?' said Lomax.

'Happened to it?' said Harcourt, briefly looking up, before beginning the second column.

'What's going on here, Harcourt? This is a damned strange place you run; everyone seems to be deaf, dumb and blind.'

'Do you mean the fire?' said Harcourt, still not looking up.

'What do you think I mean?'

Harcourt finished the second column, then turned the pencil upside down, and gripped it in the centre, between his index finger and thumb, as if it were a baton. He inspected the gold lettering on it. It was an HB. 'Lot of people, I think, feel as I do.'

'Feel as you do?'

'Yes, Lomax,' said Harcourt. 'They head for the canals, inland waterways, what have you, for peace and quiet. They don't want to get embroiled in scenes with policemen, ambulances, fire brigades. Before we know where we are, we'll be knee deep in damned newspaper people. And the television too, I shouldn't wonder. They go for these things, you know, sordid little marital squabbles.'

Lomax stared astounded at the retired army officer. 'Andrea? Where is she? Is she all right? Is she dead? What's happened to her?'

'Nasty burns, and a bit of shock. I've seen worse.'

'Oh, have you. I'm glad about that, Brigadier Harcourt, very glad.'

Harcourt looked up at him. 'Perhaps you'd like to tell me how much I owe you for draining that tank – frankly, I'd rather pay you and see you push off, than trade any more favours with you.'

'I'm holding you personally responsible for the damage to my boat,' said Lomax.

'I look after my own boats,' said Harcourt, 'and the hulls of visiting boats. Only the hulls. Not the contents. Not the misfits that inhabit them. I don't run a wet-nurse centre, nor a psychiatric unit, nor a marital advice bureau, nor,' he said, darkly, 'a safe-house for criminals on the run. I have decent people here, ordinary, decent folk; retired, mostly, ex-service people. They've had their excitement, doing something worthwhile. They don't want to wake up on Sundays and read about themselves in the tabloids.' He looked up.

'Where is she?'

'Try the College Hospital.'

'Thanks for your help,' said Lomax, with as much sarcasm as he could put into his voice.

Harcourt stared at him. 'People who play with fire get burned. Isn't that what they say?'

'Is it, Brigadier?' said Lomax, fighting back his rage. 'You spent most of your life playing with bullets, and you don't seem to have been shot.'

'Tanks, actually, Lomax.'

Lomax turned, and stormed out of the door. He heard Harcourt call out after him:

'Oh, by the way – the police would like a word with you.'
He heard the door slam shut behind him.

Lomax ran through the gloomy green hall of the decaying
Victorian building. Once it had been the mansion of a coal
baron. Now it was one of the mausoleums of the National
Health.

He found the room, on the second floor, and pushed open
the door. There were two beds, the first empty, the second
screened off. He braced himself and walked around the
screen. Andrea was lying there, her eyes closed, a protective
cage humping the bedclothes over her legs. Her right hand
lay outside the sheets, heavily bandaged. He sighed with
relief that at least her face wasn't harmed. He stood, and
looked at her. After a moment, her eyes opened. There was
recognition, but no enthusiasm.

'Hello,' he said. 'How are you?'

'I'm all right,' she said, flatly. He looked closely at her
eyes. She was heavily sedated.

'You look terrific,' he said, smiling.

'Good,' she said, her voice still flat. 'I'm glad about that.'
She moved a fraction in the bed, and raised her bandaged
hand. 'Looks worse than it is. Burns aren't easy to dress.'

'What about your body?'

'Burn on my thighs; and a bit on my chest. They say I'll be
all right in a couple of days. Got to rest.' She managed a
weak smile, but there was no warmth in it.

'What happened? Was it the Calor gas?'

'Is Calor gas about five foot two, with no front teeth?'

He stared at her. Shock and guilt swept through his body.
He tried to clear his mind, to focus. His immediate thought
was the pusher. No, impossible. He couldn't; couldn't be
going anywhere; not for a long time; even if he lived. 'A man?
Did this?'

She nodded.

'Set fire to –?'

She nodded again.

'How? Who? Who was it?'

'Safer in the marina? Safer?' she said bitterly. 'You knew, didn't you? You bloody knew.'

'What do you mean?' But in his heart, he did know.

'Money. Kept going on at me to tell the truth. The truth,' she echoed. 'Where were you? Where was the money?'

Lomax closed his eyes, and sat on the chair beside her. 'Describe him. What did he look like?'

'Leather, all in leather. And he had a match box. Shook it. Kept shaking it.' She began to cry.

'He set fire to you?'

'I woke up. There was petrol on the bedclothes.'

'Petrol?'

'One of those tins of lighter fluid. Yellow.'

'Jesus. I'm sorry. So sorry. How? How? How could he do it? Anyone? How could anyone do that?'

'You knew it was going to happen, didn't you, Max?' she said, calmly, without malice. 'You knew.'

He put his hands behind his head, and leaned down towards the floor.

'What money, Max?'

'There isn't any. There isn't any bloody money. Oh Christ, why won't anyone believe me. There isn't any bloody money!' he shouted loudly. 'I didn't take a penny. Not one damned penny.' He looked at her. 'I'm sorry. I didn't mean to shout.'

'I woke up. He was sitting there. I thought it was you,' she said, simply, helplessly. 'Then I realised he was smoking a cigarette. And you don't smoke.'

'Bastards,' he said, quietly now. 'Bastards.' He held her uninjured hand, and caressed it slowly, limply. He shook his head, backwards and forwards. 'How well did you see him?'

'Very well. He sat in front of me, on the end of the bed, for about five minutes. Horrible. He looked horrible. Smiling all the time. He was enjoying it, enjoying himself, Max.'

'Have you seen the police?'

She nodded.

'What did you say?'

'I told them I was smoking in bed, and fell asleep.'

'What?'

'I was scared; that he might come back; if I told them. That he might come after you.' She paused. 'I was scared you might have done something wrong, be in trouble with the police. I didn't think you'd be pleased with me if I told the police.'

He looked at her, gently. 'For Christ's sake, Andrea. Someone's just tried to kill you, and you want to protect me? Are you nuts?'

She smiled, a weak smile. 'I suppose I must be.'

A gong sounded.

'That the end of visiting time?'

She nodded. 'Yes.'

They sat in silence for a moment. Guilt etched away at him. 'How was your mother?' she said, suddenly.

'I didn't see her.'

'But I thought you –?'

'Family politics.' He smiled, sadly.

'You're a strange man, Max. Who are you? Who are you really?'

'I'm me.'

'Who's me?'

He shrugged.

'Don't you think I'm owed some kind of explanation?'

He heard footsteps outside. He slipped off the chair and put his head out into the corridor. 'I was right. People are leaving. Do you want anything? Magazines? Fruit?'

'I want an explanation, Max.'

'Not now. I will explain. I'll try, anyway.'

'I'm frightened, Max. Frightened he might come back. He said he would. Come back for me. If you didn't give him the money.'

'I don't even know who the hell he is. I'll tell you one thing: I'm going to find out. And when I do, he won't come back.'

Suddenly, her eyes bulged, her face became sheet white, and she began to scream, hysterically.

'Calm down. I'll stay here. I'll protect you.'

She screamed even louder. He heard footsteps, running.

He turned round. A nurse ran in the room. 'What's the matter?'

She continued screaming.

'A nightmare, nurse. She just woke up. A nightmare.'

'I'll get Sister. Give her an injection.' The nurse ran out.

'Him, he, him!' She gasped, panting, wildly. 'In the door, his head, he just came in the door!'

'What do you mean? Calm down, calm down!'

'Just then, just then. I saw him. A second ago!' She took massive gulps. 'His head, poked, poked his head, round the door. Ran. Ran off.'

'Are you serious?'

'I am. Oh God, I am. Leather jacket. It was him. It was him!'

Lomax flung himself out of the door, and down the corridor. It was crowded with departing visitors. He looked desperately for signs of a leather jacket. He crashed past the people, pushed a trolley out of the way, barged through a pair of swinging doors, narrowly missing a nurse with a tray of instruments.

'Sorry,' he said, and sprinted on, deaf to her admonishment.

He hurled himself down the staircase, too fast to stop for the two doctors coming up abreast, and crashed through them. He skidded round the corner, and down the next flight. The downstairs hallway was thick with visitors. He pushed past them, looking, looking all the time, for the leather jacket, for other exits. He reached the main exit. It was blocked by a family gathering. He moved sideways. They moved sideways. He moved the other way. Three people came in the door. 'For Christ's sake!' he shouted, physically levering a couple, who were shaking hands, apart, and flung himself through the revolving doors.

He scanned the car park. Heard a car door slam; another; suddenly, the crackle of a motorbike starting. It stalled. He broke into a sprint. It started again. 250cc, or thereabouts. He had heard it before; by the canal; the same damned engine. He tore across the car park. The man in leather on

71

the blue machine raced out in front of him, heeling over, accelerating furiously.

Lomax tried to head him off, but the machine was already travelling at high speed. A couple dragged their small boy out of the way, as the motorcycle tore over the spot where the child had been standing, and out through the main gates. Lomax dived over the wall, as the bike heeled out into the traffic. He locked his eyes on the rear number plate. ADF 937 Y. ADF 937 Y. He fixed the number into his memory. DF. Cheshire plate. 'I'll get you, you bastard,' he said. 'I'll get you.'

CHAPTER ELEVEN

The pips began to shriek at him, and he shoved in the ten pence coin. 'I'd like to speak to Sergeant Bramwell,' said Lomax.

There was a pause. 'Do you mean *Inspector* Bramwell?'

'Inspector Barbara Bramwell?' he said, tentatively.

'I'll put you through.'

There was a long pause, and he pushed in a second coin. There was a voice at the other end when the clacking stopped.

'Hello?' said the female voice, tough, no-nonsense. 'Inspector Bramwell.'

He had no idea what kind of a reception to expect. 'Barbara – It's Max.'

'Max!' The response came back instantaneously; happily. 'Max!'

'How are you?'

'I'm fine. What a surprise! Where are you?'

'Up here. I'm at the College Hospital at the moment.'

'Are you ill?'

'Visiting.'

'I didn't realise you were out yet.'

'I was a good boy. Full remission. You don't mind talking to me?'

'Why on earth not?'

'I didn't exactly get welcomed back to London with ticker tape and bunting.'

There was a pause. 'No,' she said heavily, and paused. 'Why, Max?' she said. 'Why the hell did you do it?'

73

'Not you too?' he said.

'What do you mean?'

'I don't know,' he said. 'I thought – maybe if there was one person who might have – believed –'

'Why the hell didn't you ever come and talk to me about it?'

Lomax paused. 'I don't know. Got drained, I suppose; drained by the whole damned thing. In the end, I just let them beat me.'

'Not easily from what I heard.'

Lomax smiled, sadly. 'No. Not easily.'

'You want to come round? Have a drink?'

Lomax looked over his shoulder, at the drab green walls of the hospital, at an old woman, with sheet white hair, and an even whiter face, being carried in on a stretcher. He looked at the empty seats, and the few occupied seats, a fretting woman, walking up and down, smoking, one drag after another. Another woman, sitting holding a cloth over a child's eye. 'No more visitors,' the ward sister had told him adamantly. Not until eleven o'clock tomorrow. Andrea had been sedated; she was still suffering seriously from shock. Andrea was being wheeled into a large ward at the moment, as her room was needed for someone more seriously ill. She would be safe in an open ward, at any rate, surrounded by people. There was nothing he could usefully do here. 'Sure,' said Lomax into the phone. 'What time do you get off?'

'I'll be home by eight.'

'Same place?'

'Some of us lead normal lives.'

She looked much the same, as she opened the front door of her flat; a little fatter, perhaps, and her brown hair was cut short. It suited her, he thought. 'Good evening,' he said, and then added, with emphasis, 'Inspector!'

'Max!' She leaned forward, gave him a long kiss on the lips, hugged him tightly, then slid her hands down into the rear pockets of his jeans. 'Hallo, you big brute.'

'Hallo, you little brute.'

74

'Fat little brute. Fatter and older.'

Lomax felt a hand pull out of his trouser pocket, slide down inside the front of his trousers, and cold fingers curl around his genitals.

'Bloody hell,' he said. 'Cold hands.'

'Warm heart.'

'Oh yes.'

'Just checking your Barbarometer.'

'Rising,' he said.

'Got a long way to go.'

'Any chance of a drink?' he said.

'You came all this way just for a drink?' The hand slipped out of his trousers.

'You look terrific,' he said.

'You think so? I'm getting fat, old, and wrinkled, and my bust is getting smaller. But you've got better looking, you swine. Men have all the luck. Particularly you, Max. You've always been a lucky sod.'

From the look on his face, she knew she'd said the wrong thing. 'I'm sorry. I didn't mean that. You know what I mean. Come in. What would you like? Whisky? Gin? Wine? Have you eaten?'

'Whisky – and a drop of water; be fine.' He walked through into the living room, glancing curiously round, out of habit, looking for signs of change, other men. But everything was exactly as he remembered it. Then he noticed a photograph, on the window sill; Barbara was looking tanned, sitting on the stern of a yacht.

'Where was that?' he nodded, as she brought the whisky through.

'Cowes. Last year.'

'Cowes? Bit flash?'

'Yes,' she said, wistfully. 'Didn't last. Kinky sod. Could only do it when I was in uniform.' She laughed, a laugh full of regret but no bitterness. 'And I thought he was Mister Right.'

Lomax felt sorry, in a way, for Barbara. She would dearly like to marry, and yet none of her relationships with men ever turned out successful. He had the feeling that secretly, she hoped one day that their own relationship might go beyond the purely casual basis on which it had been for – it must be nearly ten years, he thought, but at the same time, he knew, she was realistic enough to expect nothing.

She sat down on the sofa beside him.

'Inspector,' he said. 'Inspector Bramwell.'

'Sounds a bit butch, don't you think?' she said.

'Sounds a damned sight better than "Ex-Drugs Squad",' he said, with a trace of bitterness.

'So what happened, Max? What happened?'

'What do the tom-toms say in your neck of the jungle?'

'They say that Uncle Max pulled a smart stunt. That he's stashed away one hundred gorillas in old folding, and that two years was a cheap price to pay. Lot of pissed off people, Max. Some envious, the young ones. Some bitter, the old hands; disgracing the name of the police, and all that. But mostly jealousy, I'd say.'

'I didn't think I had too many friends left in the Force.'

'No. I don't think you have.'

'I was quite surprised you were prepared to talk to me. Wouldn't do your career any good if I was spotted here.'

'I don't think this is Moscow, quite yet.'

He smiled.

'So tell me. The Alan Lomax story?'

He sipped his whisky. 'There's not much to tell.' He looked at the white rug that lay on the carpet. 'I didn't do it.'

She looked at him. 'You've suffered, haven't you? You really have.'

'Glad you noticed.'

'You've aged, Max.'

'Thanks a lot.'

'Suits you. You've always had almost' – she paused – 'almost a baby face. Innocent. Now it's not innocent any more. There's a bit of meanness there now.'

'Don't stop. Keep going.'

She giggled.

'Do you believe I didn't do it?'

'Max. If you tell me you didn't do it, you didn't do it. But it wouldn't make any difference to me if you had done it.'

'What do you mean?'

She gave him a kiss. 'You've always been a bastard. Might as well be a rich bastard!'

'Thanks a lot.'

'Tell me the whole story.'

He shrugged. 'I was stitched.' He turned the glass around in his hands. 'You knew a bit about the case, didn't you?'

She nodded.

'Eighteen months we'd been on it. Six of us. Stratton. Dixie Dean. Reynolds. Dave Brabrook. Myself. And Pember. Neil Pember. Reckon those bastards were putting a couple of million quid of smack on the London streets a year. We had them. We had those bastards. Taped. Bloody taped. Muggins here had to make the drop. One hundred long ones in used notes in an old Samsonite. It was all there. Couldn't risk a substitute. I was going to hand over the money, they were going to hand over the goods. Sat in the back of their car; remember them opening the case. Newspapers. Nothing but bloody newspapers.' He took a long pull on his drink.

'Your newsagent testified that you'd ordered fifty copies of the *Evening Standard.*'

He smiled. 'Someone ordered them. In my name. Asked for them to be delivered to my door. They were delivered. But I never bloody saw them.'

'You going to try to clear your name?'

He took another pull of his drink. 'I can feel the wall of silence clamped all around me. CID in Fulham tried to run me out of town the day I was released. Nobody wants to know. Don't want skeletons being flushed out of closets; shake up too much dust. Yes, I want to clear my name. For Steve's sake, if nothing else.'

'How is Steve?'

He laughed, bitterly. 'I don't know. I'm trying to find him.' He smiled, sadly. 'Seems like prison was the easy part.'

'If I can help you in any way –'

'Thanks.' He shrugged. 'Not worth it. You're doing well. Could end up as the first female Commissioner.'

She laughed. 'Doubt it. I don't play the game well enough.' Then she paused. 'Who were you visiting in hospital? Grim hospital that.'

'I know. A friend.'

'Ill?'

'Accident. On a boat.'

'Dangerous places, the canals.'

'Yes. Never know when you might get eaten by a frog.'

She laughed, then her face became serious again. 'What do you want, Max. You didn't come all the way here just to shoot the breeze, I can tell.'

He smiled. 'I want a small favour. I want you to do something for me.'

She pulled down his zip.

'Not that!'

'How were the birds in jail?'

'There weren't any.' He winced. 'God, your hands are cold.'

'I thought cons these days had everything well organised.'

'Barbara!' A sudden warmth replaced the cold.

'Two years inside has done him some good too!'

'A licence number. I want it checked out.'

'Not right at the moment,' she murmured. 'I'm busy.'

CHAPTER TWELVE

'Nasty things, fires on boats,' said the short, tubby boat-yard owner, Jimmy Hurst, carefully drawing the paint brush down the wall. He stood back to admire his handiwork, and wiped a blob of paint off his vast belly, which hung over the belt of his grubby shorts in neatly layered folds.

'I'm not crazy about them anywhere,' said Lomax.

'It's the smell that's worst. You can never get rid of the smell.' He mopped his bald pate, smearing paint on to that too. 'That's better. Looks like new.'

'She's needed a spruce up for a while,' said Lomax. 'At least this has made me get on with it.' He jammed his brush into the pot of turps. 'That's about it. How about a beer?'

'Wouldn't say no.'

Lomax pulled two beer cans out of the fridge and they went up into the cockpit. He pulled the ring of one and handed it to the boat-yard owner. 'Ever come across Harcourt, Brigadier Harcourt?' he said, with an exaggerated military accent.

'Up the canal? Harcourt Marina?'

'The very same.'

'Wanker. Calls himself a brigadier. I heard he was a captain, drummed out of the army for selling groceries to the krauts.'

'Doesn't entirely surprise me.'

'Friend of yours?'

'Not exactly.' Lomax opened his own beer and sat down.

'Now that's what I call a piece of crumpet,' said the boat-yard owner.

Lomax watched a moorhen paddle past.

'Class too,' said Hurst, pulling the beer can from his lips and ogling.

Lomax looked around, following Hurst's gaze. A girl was paying a taxi, in the boat-yard entrance.

'Andrea!' he said.

'Not one of your harem, Max?'

'Yes. The pyromaniac.'

Lomax jumped ashore and ran over to her. She stood, holding a plastic carrier bag. 'Andrea! Hallo!' He gave her a kiss on the cheek. 'What are you doing? I was going to collect you.'

'They discharged me early. Said I was fine.'

'How are you?' He looked down at her hand. There was a wide strip of Elastoplast.

'I'm all right; fine. They said it was more shock than anything.'

'I was going to come and get you, tomorrow.'

'Mr. Lomax?' Hurst's assistant, Eric, stuck his head out of the office. 'There's a phone call for you.'

'Thanks.' He turned to Andrea. 'Won't be a sec.'

He walked in and picked up the receiver.

'Hallo, Sailor,' said the voice.

'Barbara. Hi!'

'Listen – I've got to be quick – I'm wanted on a call-out. I've got some information. That number.'

'Yes?'

'Belongs to a man called Naylor. Dennis Charles Naylor. Know him?'

'No.'

'46, Addison Road, Northwich. Married; no children.'

'Any record?'

'Oh yes, he's got form.'

'Like what?'

'Three stretches. Four months G.B.H. That was five years ago. Eighteen months, demanding money with menaces. Came out five months ago.'

'Oh yes?'

'Small time bully boy. Protection merchant. Gaming machine circuit round the Liverpool area.' She paused. 'Oh, and by the way, he likes to burn people.'

'So I've noticed.'

'You've noticed?'

'Doesn't matter. Not important.'

'Watch him, Max. He's nasty.'

'Sounds a real sweetheart. Is he tooled up?'

'Probably.'

'You're twenty-four carat.'

'And you're a sod.'

'Yeah, well, we've all got our cross to bear.'

'Give me a call later – I might have something for you on that other matter.'

'Other matter?'

'You wanted a hot tip? For your journalist friend? Something good? Remember?'

'Yes? Got something?'

'I will have. It'll cost you.'

'How much?'

'At least a whole night.'

'You're a hard negotiator.'

'I'm not, Max. That's my problem. Take care. Don't get eaten by any frogs.'

'I'll try and keep clear of them. Take care.' He hung up and walked out of the office.

'What does "tooled up" mean?'

Lomax flushed, not realising Andrea had been standing so close to the door. He took her by the arm and led her out of earshot of Eric, towards the boat. 'It means carrying a gun.'

'A gun?' she said, surprised at first; then she looked at him, silently.

'Slang,' said Lomax.

'Whose slang?'

He shrugged. 'Just slang.'

'You lead a weird old life, don't you, Max? Midnight visitors spraying your guests with petrol. Guns. Who do you work for?'

'The Moonies,' he said.

She smiled, grudgingly. 'Who's the fellow on your boat? Your minder?'

'That there man owns the very ground on which you are now walking.' He paused, and called, loudly. 'Hey, Shortie, stand up and meet a real lady.'

'I am standing up, you cheeky sod,' said Hurst, with a broad smile. He held out his arm, and shook her hand, careful not to press the burn. 'Pleased to meet you – never met a real live pyromaniac before.' The grin froze on his face and slowly turned to a frown, as he realised she was not amused. 'Better be getting along,' he said. 'Er – nice meeting you – Miss – er Mrs – er – thanks for the beer, Max.'

'Pleasure. Thanks for you help.'

'Thanks a lot,' she turned to Lomax, furiously, as soon as Hurst was a safe distance away. 'Pyromaniac indeed.'

'It was your idea in the first place.'

'I don't need it made into a joke.'

'I'm sorry,' he said. He jumped on to the boat, and took her hand, to help her on board. She lifted up her leg and winced.

'Ouch.'

He looked, worried, at her leg. 'Painful?'

'Yes. It's sore. That's where the worst burn is; bit of burning sheet stuck to it as I got out of the bed.'

'I really am sorry. I didn't know.'

'I'll have a nice little scar there, but it won't show, as long as I don't wear a mini-skirt, and I think I'm a bit old for those anyway. I smell paint.'

'Yes. Jimmy's been helping me.'

'How bad was the damage?'

'Could have been worse. I still have a boat.'

'Can I look?'

'Paint's still wet; best wait an hour or two. Like a drink?'

'Tell you what I fancy: a nice cold shandy.'

'I'll see what I can find.' He paused. 'I usually keep some on board for Steve.'

Lomax went below, and came up a few minutes later,

holding a glass. 'Only one can, I'm afraid.'

'That looks great.'

He handed her the glass, picked up his beer can. 'Cheers.' He took a long pull on the beer, and sat down.

'Who's tooled up, Max?'

He looked at her and said nothing for a moment. A glint of light caught his eye, and he looked up, instinctively. It came from one of the windows of the Bridge Inn, a couple of hundred yards down on the other side of the canal.

'My friend? Is it him?'

Lomax looked at her. 'Might be.'

The colour drained from her face. 'I see.'

He saw the glint again. Third window from left, first floor, he watched without moving his head. 'I'm going inside. You won't see me for about ten minutes. Don't look puzzled, and don't move. I want you just to keep on talking to me, although I won't reply. Can you do that?'

'But what on –'

'Be a good girl,' he said, sauntering casually through the hatch.

'Max?'

'Yes?'

'What shall I talk about?'

'Anything that comes into your head.'

'Like what a shit you are?'

'That'll do nicely.' He walked through the galley, through the saloon, into his bedroom. There was a hatch beyond his bedroom to the front of the boat, which would be concealed from the hotel window by the cabin roof. He crouched down, and crawled out of the for'ard hatch into the cockpit. He eased himself over the deck rail, and lowered himself gently down into the oily, dirty water between the prow of his boat and the bank. He checked there was nothing coming down the canal, eyed his mark on the opposite bank, took in a massive lungful of air, then duck-dived under his boat, and swam, as hard as he could, across the bottom of the canal, until his hands plunged into the oozing mud on the far side.

He surfaced, wiped the water from his eyes, and looked

up. He was hidden from the window by a pile of crates. He looked across at *Harmony*. Andrea was sitting, talking into the empty hatch, and hadn't noticed him. He hauled himself up on to the bank, and crouching low, ran around the pile of crates, up to the wall of the inn, and then began to walk around to the front entrance.

He stopped, tipped some water out of his plimsolls, then walked in. There was no one behind the front desk, but he saw an old woman arranging flowers in the dining room. She looked across at him, quizzically.

'Fell in!' he said, jovially.

She nodded, turning back to her flowers.

He sprinted up to the first floor. There were five doors on the canal side. He walked up to the middle one and knocked, firmly.

There was a pause, and then a voice. 'Who is it?'

'Room service,' said Lomax.

There was another pause and then the door began to open. A short man, face red with the veins of a heavy drinker, blinked at him, in stupefied recognition. Over his shoulder, Lomax saw a camera with a long lens resting on a table by the open window.

'I came about a passport photo,' said Lomax, then he rammed his knee, hard, up between the man's legs. The man doubled up in pain, gasping at the air.

'Sorry,' said Lomax. 'It's my nervous twitch.' He shut the door behind him, locked it, and put the key in his pocket. The man sank down on to the floor, head stretching down towards his knees.

Lomax walked across to the camera, and picked it up. He studied it carefully for a moment. 'F8,' he said. 'Two-fifty. ASA 400. Not taking family portraits, are you, that's for sure.' He flipped open the back of the camera, and tore the film out. 'Oh blast,' he said, 'now look what's happened.'

The man stared at him, eyes goggling in fear and pain.

'Nice cameras, Nikons,' said Lomax. 'Hear you can drop them from a great height.' He laid it gently back on the table. 'Used to be a bit of a photographer myself. Nothing fancy, know what I mean? Family snaps; the odd sunset. Never had anything quite as flash as this. Five hundred mill; tell the sex of a mosquito at a hundred yards.' He paused, and walked over to where a photographic bag was lying on the floor. He turned it upside down, and four films clattered to the floor. 'Been a busy boy, haven't you? Entomologist, are you? Or an ornithologist?'

'Not those, please!' the man gasped out.

Lomax looked at him with an expression of contempt. 'Why not?'

The man's jacket was hanging on a chair. He walked over to it. The photographer started, as if to get up.

'Don't bother to get up,' said Lomax. 'I don't want to have to knock you down again. I'm sure you're just some poor dumb bastard trying to do a day's work.' He tugged the man's wallet out of his jacket and flicked it open. He tugged out a press pass. 'Joe Walker,' it said. He slipped it back, and replaced the wallet in the jacket. 'An underpaid day's work at that,' said Lomax. He stamped in turn on each of the four exposed film reels, shattering the plastic covering, then unspooled the films. He held one up. 'Could put jam on this, Joe. Make good fly paper. Remember the old fly paper, Joe? Flit made that obsolete, didn't it.' Lomax raised his fist, clenched around an imaginary can of Flit, pressed his thumb on the imaginary plunger, and sprayed imaginary flies around the room. 'Good stuff, Flit,' he said. 'Get rid of almost any vermin. Might even work on press photographers. How's my friend Robinson?'

The photographer looked at him without commenting.

'Bad hearing, have you?'

'He's all right.'

'You must give him my regards.' Lomax walked over to the window and looked out. He could see Andrea, still sitting on the rear deck, talking through the hatchway. 'Got a short memory, Robinson, that's his problem. And a thick skin. Keeps forgetting I don't like being followed, don't like being snooped on. Perhaps you'll be a good fellow and remind him, Joe?'

85

The photographer looked up at him, and said nothing.

'Otherwise,' said Lomax, 'I'll be back.' He sprayed the imaginary Flit gun again, then let himself out of the door, locked it from the outside, and walked back downstairs. He put the key on the reception desk, and walked out of the main entrance.

'Rhubarb,' said Andrea, as he walked quietly up behind her. 'Rhubarb, rhubarb, bloody rhubarb.'

'Doesn't grow too well on boats,' he said.

She spun around. 'God, you gave me a fright. What the hell's happened to you? You're sopping wet.'

'Had a shower.'

'In your clothes?'

'Doesn't everyone?'

'What is going on? You're the weirdest person I've ever met. What is this stupid game of yours?'

Lomax sat down beside her. 'There's a lovely hotel in the village; does the world's best fillet steak, char grilled, all the trimmings.'

'Thanks,' she said. 'I've had enough of char grills for one week.'

He picked up his beer can, and toyed with it. 'Don't be mad at me,' he said. 'The whole world's mad at me.'

'So it seems.'

'There are some nice clothes shops in the village. Get you a nice outfit.'

'I'm quite happy with the outfits I've got, in my suitcase.'

Lomax looked at her, got up and went into the cabin. A minute later he came out, holding the charred skeleton of a suitcase in his hand. He looked at her quizzically.

'Any shops in the village sell suitcases?' she said.

CHAPTER THIRTEEN

'Were you really going to come and collect me?'

'Yes.'

'Thank you; that's nice.' She took his hand and squeezed it hard, as they walked across the boat-yard. She paused for a moment. 'How were you going to – come – you don't have a car, do you?'

He dug his hand in his pocket and held up a set of car keys. He pointed at an elderly and battered Vauxhall, parked between two boats on cradles, towards which they were walking.

He opened the door for her and then climbed in the driver's side. 'Belongs to Jimmy,' he explained. 'Hardly uses it; always lets me borrow it.' He started the engine and they pulled out into the road. A few hundred yards down, he stopped at a newsagents, and dashed in.

He came out a couple of minutes later, holding a paper bag, and got back into the car.

'What did you go in there for?' she asked.

'Cancel the papers,' he said, deadpan.

Andrea looked at him, trying to work out whether he was joking or not. 'You're funny,' she said, after a moment.

'Am I?'

'Yes. I can never work out what you're going to do next.'

'Would you like me to write out a schedule and pin it on the wall?'

'At least I'd know where I was.'

He overtook a crocodile of cyclists. 'You're in Higher Walton – kind of village. We are about to stop at a parade of shops, where you might find a nice new outfit or two, and possibly a suitcase. I also have a little shopping to do. Afterwards, we are going to a hotel I know, where I am going to treat you to one of the best dinners you'll ever have up these parts.' He studied the rearview mirror, carefully. The road behind was clear.

'Sounds good,' she said. 'What happens then?'

He pulled the car up, and began to reverse into a parking bay.

'I'll probably hold your hand and whisper sweet nothings into your ear.'

'You didn't tell me you'd booked a room here?' She followed him into the vast bedroom.

'You didn't ask.'

'You said you would hold my hand and whisper sweet nothings into my ear.'

He took her hand, gently. 'Rhubarb,' he whispered. 'Rhubarb, rhubarb, rhubarb.'

'Bastard! She punched him playfully, then jumped back on to the massive bed. 'A four-poster. I've never slept in a four-poster. This is a treat. Thank you, Max. You were right about the meal. The carrots; they were incredible. Wish I could cook steak like that. I can never get it black on the outside and red in the middle – it always comes out a sort of murky brown all over.' She kicked her shoes off. 'Do you think I was greedy having two sweets? Raspberries and meringue – mmmn. Heaven. And I just can't resist trifle. Impossible. How do they get it so creamy? Think I'm going to have trifle for breakfast.' She paused and the tone of her voice changed. 'What are you doing, Max?'

'I have to go out.'

'Oh no. Max, no!'

'I won't be long.'

'Where are you going?'

'I won't be long. Promise.'

'It's ten o'clock! How the hell can you go out at ten o'clock?'

'I'll tell you when I get back.'

'I won't be here when you get back.'

'Where are you going to go at ten o'clock at night in Higher Walton?'

'Where the hell are you going to go? To some bird?'

He shook his head. 'Please, Andrea. It is important, believe me.'

'Believe you? Max, I don't want to be alone; not at the moment. I'm frightened. Can't you understand that?'

He walked over and sat down beside her. 'That's why I have to go out.'

Her eyes opened wide. 'That phone call – tooled up. Is that where you're going?'

He stood up. 'Stay here, Andrea. Please. Don't go out. Don't answer the door, to anyone. Anyone at all. I'll be back as quickly as I can.'

He watched her as he left, staring at him through frightened eyes. He gave her a reassuring smile, and closed the door.

When he reached the foyer of the hotel, he looked around carefully. He went outside, and walked around the area, carefully, doubling back on his tracks twice, checking parked cars. Finally, he was satisfied. He went back into the hotel car park for the third time, and got into the Vauxhall. From his pocket, he pulled a crumpled paper bag. He pulled out a cellophane-wrapped cigar and a box of matches. From another pocket, he pulled out a yellow Ronson's lighter fuel can. He shook the can, a couple of times, testing, then put it back into his pocket. He removed the cellophane from the cigar, crammed it into the car's ashtray, then stuck the cigar inside his sock. He shook the box of matches, gently, removed some matches, then shook it again. It gave a more pronounced rattle, this time. He took out a couple more and shook again. Now he was satisfied. He started the car, drove out of the car park, and headed off down the road, looking for the first signpost to Northwich.

There weren't many people to ask, in Northwich, at eleven-thirty on a Thursday night, and most of those that were around had been too busy blowing their pay packets in the boozers to be able to remember where Addison Road might be, even if they had ever known. The fourth man Lomax stopped was even drunker than the rest. He gazed at Lomax, helplessly, fumbling and stuttering. 'Know it,' he said. 'Aye, know it I do. Don't go. It'll come. Not far from here. I do know it. I do definitely know it. Addison.' He enlisted the physical support of a lamp post, and studied it for a moment, intently, as if he had never seen one before. 'Addison. Aye. Knew I knew it; course I bloody know it. I live there myself!'

Addison Road was a Victorian terrace, overlooked by a gasometer on one side, and by a railway embankment on the other. A train came past, and the noise was deafening. Lomax smiled to himself. He drove the length of the road, saw number 46, but carried on past. He turned down the first side road, and parked.

He walked back to 46. Fortunately the street lighting was poor, and he didn't feel conspicuous. There was a light on in the front room, and Lomax walked quietly up, peering through a gap in the curtains. A man was lying in an armchair. A weasely man, with a greasy face, and short black hair unevenly cut. He was sleeping, heavily, in front of the television. On the screen a fist fight was in progress. Suddenly, the man woke up. He looked over his shoulder and called out. A moment later, an upstairs light came on, and Lomax heard the sound of curtains being pulled. The man looked at the screen, smiled at the sight, and his eyelids closed again.

Lomax heard footsteps, and knelt down low. A man walked his dog past the house. He heard the man stop, heard a short burst of trickling water, and then footsteps again. He saw the man in the chair, whom he presumed to be Naylor, wake up again, shout what was clearly a reply to the same question, and then fall asleep again.

It was half an hour before Naylor went up to bed, slowly, dragging his feet. The bright light came on upstairs, stayed on for ten minutes, then went off again. It was half past midnight, and the house was dark. Lomax pulled a pair of gloves out of his pocket and put them on. Putting his hands in his pockets, he walked out of the garden, and back down the road, to the turning where he had parked. Opposite his car, was a twitten, and he walked down it, along the back of the Addison Road houses. A small dog began to yap somewhere, and was then silenced. Counting carefully, he stopped at what he reckoned was Naylor's house. There was a gate through, but he did not want to risk making any sound, so he hauled himself over it, and jumped softly down on to a patch of rough grass and weeds.

He peered into a small shed. Something glinted in there; a motorcycle. He walked around the shed, until he came to another window at the rear. Looking through, he could just make out the number plate. It confirmed all he needed to know. He walked silently up to a lop-sided extension attached to the house, and walked around, studying the windows. They were hinged vertically, and in poor condition.

He looked carefully through the glass for signs of movement, then walked across, and peered through another window, on to a small dining alcove. There was no sound of any movement, and he walked back to the kitchen window. He pulled a plastic dart with a rubber suction cup from his pocket, licked the tip, then pressed it against the pane of the hinged window. Then he pulled out his glass cutter, and cut a circle, a little bigger than his fist, in the glass around the dart. He carefully put the cutter back into his anorak, and zipped the pocket shut. Then he waited, silently.

More than twenty minutes passed, and he began to wonder if perhaps there weren't going to be any more tonight. Then, suddenly, he heard the sound. Or was he imagining it? No, he knew, suddenly, as the clanking and rattling became louder; it was a train, and it was going to come past. He waited until the sound had built up into a crescendo, then holding the dart firmly in one hand, he gave the glass a sharp punch with the other. The circle came away cleanly, and he pulled it out, through the gap it had made, prised off the rubber suction cup, and put the dart back in the same pocket as the cutter.

Then he slipped his hand in through the hole, tugged up the window lever, and gently opened the window. It was a long train, still rattling past, and he was grateful for it, as he heaved himself up over the window ledge, then down on to the table the other side of it, sending a vase crashing to the floor in the process; but the noise of the train completely drowned the sound.

He slipped through the kitchen, into the hall, feeling the ground carefully with his feet for turned-up carpets or sudden steps. There was a strong smell of fresh paint, as if the house had recently been decorated. His feet trod in something soft, slippery; he looked down, and felt the floor; it was a dust sheet.

He tested the bottom stair carefully, and began to climb, very slowly, testing each stair in turn, keeping his hand well away from the banisters which had felt rickety.

A board groaned at the top. Lomax froze, moved his foot, tried again. It groaned louder. He waited, listening for any sound of movement. But there was none. He pressed himself hard up against the wall, where the boards would be their most secure, and put his foot forward again. This time there was no sound, and he began to ease his way along the landing, keeping his feet wide apart now, on the outside edge of the floor.

He reached a door, and turned the handle, slowly. There was a slight clank. He stopped, turned it further, then began to push. The door resisted at first, then slowly moved forward, still with a lot of resistance, and a hissing sound, as it slid through the heavy pile of a new carpet. The smell of new nylon hit his nostrils, followed by a waft of cold air, and he saw the curtains flutter in the draught. He stepped into the room, and pushed the door closed behind him as quickly as he dared. Then he stood still and listened to the sound of heavy breathing. Two distinct rhythms. One quiet, with deep draughts of air. The other long, slow, slightly congested, and a slight gargling sound with each exhalation. They were both heavily asleep, he thought, with relief.

He slipped noiselessly across past the bottom of the bed, to where the breathing was coming from, and looked down at the sleeping figure of Naylor. He eased his glove off, putting it carefully into his pocket, then slowly and gently moved his hand underneath Naylor's pillow. The tips of his fingers felt something cold, hard, but the position of Naylor's head was such that he couldn't get his fingers further around it. With his free hand, he gently tapped the shoulder of Naylor that was nearest his wife. There was a momentary break in Naylor's breathing rhythm, as he began to roll over. As he rolled, Lomax pulled the gun out from under the pillow, and stood, waiting; almost immediately, the rhythm was restored.

Lomax pushed the revolver into his jacket pocket, then pulled out the can of Ronson's lighter fluid. He flipped up the red nipple, then slowly emptied the contents over the bedclothes. Then he carefully placed the empty tin on Naylor's bedside table. He picked up a chair, removed the clothes that were strewn over it, and carried the chair close to the bed. He sat down, tugged the cigar out of his sock, and put it in his mouth. He pulled out the box of matches, struck one and lit his cigar. He inhaled deeply, surprising himself at how good it tasted after so long, and conscious that it made him, for a moment, feel quite light-headed. He exhaled, blowing out the match, which he put on the floor beside him. Naylor's wife stirred. 'Den?' she said, puzzled. 'Den?'

Lomax took another long drag, watching the bright red glow of the tip of the cigar.

'What on earth you doing, Den?'

Lomax exhaled.

There was a sudden sharp scream from Mrs Naylor, then her voice became hushed. 'Den,' she whispered. 'Den, for God's sake wake up!'

'Wassermarrer?'

'Who are you? Who are you?' she said, twice.

'Leave off, Ren, I'm tired.'

'There's someone in the room.'

Lomax heard the sound of heavy sniffing; he smiled to himself, taking another long drag.

'I can smell a cigar,' said Naylor. 'You gone mad or something? Smoking cigars? In bed?'

'It's not me,' she hissed. 'There's someone –' her voice began to get hysterical. 'Someone in the room!'

Lomax heard the heaving of bedclothes, then the sound of a hand groping. There was a clank, which sounded like the lighter fluid tin, then more scrabbling, then a click, and a bright bedside light came on.

'Aaaaagh!' Ren Naylor shrieked in fright.

Lomax smiled politely, as the woman, white face accentuated by cold cream, hair in tight curlers, tried to sit up. He took another drag.

Naylor blinked at him, stupefied and still not fully awake. 'Who the hell are you?'

'Evening, Mr Naylor,' said Lomax, courteously. 'Evening, Mrs Naylor.'

'Call the police,' she said.

'Shut up,' said Naylor, waking up fast.

'Who are you?' she said.

Lomax studied the ash on the end of the cigar. 'Tell her, Naylor. Tell her who I am.'

Naylor looked at him, brain whirring.

Lomax nodded, encouragingly.

'Name's Lomax,' said Naylor.

She stared at him, trembling, uncomprehending. 'What – what do you want?' she said, faltering.

'An ashtray?' ventured Lomax.

'Haven't got one – not here – not in here.'

'Pity,' he said, flicking the ash off the cigar and on to the carpet.

She kept her eyes transfixed on Lomax, then suddenly began to move her hand about. 'Here, the bed's wet; all damp.'

Naylor, too, kept his eyes on Lomax, but began to pat around with his hands. 'Jesus,' he said, as it began to dawn.

Lomax slowly and deliberately pulled the match box out

of his pocket, and shook it hard, a couple of times. The matches rattled loudly.

'Den, he's a nutter. That's what he is.'

'Shut up,' said Naylor.

'Bought you a little prezzie, Naylor,' said Lomax, pointing to the Ronson can.

Naylor looked at it, nervously.

'Never know when you might need it, eh? Never know when you might suddenly get taken with that wild, burning desire, eh, Naylor? To go and set light to the odd church, eh? The odd warehouse, eh? The odd houseboat, eh?'

Naylor whipped his arm under his pillow, groped frantically, then looked back at Lomax, straight down the barrel of his own gun.

'Don't want to leave shooters lying around, Naylor; very careless,' said Lomax.

'What do you want?' said Naylor.

'Want?' he said, quizzically. 'I just happened to be passing. Thought I'd drop in, shoot the breeze. Know what I mean?'

Naylor glared, his mind racing.

'Big man, your husband, Mrs Naylor, but not a very nice one. Not a nice one at all. Think about changing him, if I were you. Know what he likes doing?'

She continued to stare at him.

'He likes tipping petrol over people's beds.'

'Petrol –?' Suddenly, her face turned even whiter, and her mouth hung open, trembling.

Lomax smiled, and rattled the match box, gently, but firmly. 'Yes, petrol. Uses it on people – when they don't co-operate, don't give him what he wants. Young girls, those sort of people.' He paused. 'Well, you look surprised. Didn't he tell you? Petrol all over them, then he sets them on fire.' He paused. 'Suppose it's not the sort of thing you tell your old lady.'

Naylor began to sweat.

'You're looking warm, Dennis. Feeling warm, are you?'

Naylor looked at him, face screwed up in fear.

''Cause it's nothing to how warm you're going to feel in a

minute.' Lomax smiled, took another long drag on his cigar, and studied the burning tip. 'Thought you wanted to see me. Isn't that why you set fire to my bird?' He looked at Mrs Naylor, and registered the bewilderment on her face.

Naylor said nothing.

'You gone awful quiet, Naylor. Heat not agree with you?'

Naylor continued to say nothing.

'Small matter of a hundred grand, I hear you were interested in. Lot of bread that. Where do you suppose a fellow like myself would get that kind of money?'

'It – it was in the newspapers,' said Naylor, trembling.

'Written all over her tits on page three of the *Sun*, was it?'

'Not the *Sun*; didn't see it in the *Sun* –' Naylor was blurting now, eager to please. That was what Lomax wanted.

'Who you working for, Naylor? Who sent you?'

'No one. I work for meself.'

'Not what I've heard. Not what an amusement arcade manager told me,' lied Lomax.

'Well – I got a job, yeah, debt collector.'

'Debt collector. So who do I owe?'

'No one. You don't owe no one.'

'Some people might not agree with you.'

Naylor began to smile, earnestly, trying to charm Lomax now. 'Well, I wouldn't know about that. Course I wouldn't. I got no axe to grind.'

'Haven't you?' said Lomax. 'You go around setting fire to women when you've no axe to grind. What do you do when you have an axe to grind? Who you working for, Naylor?'

'I told you. No one.'

'I don't believe you, Naylor. I don't believe you, and I can't wait much longer. Don't want to miss the last train.' He rattled the box of matches.

'Den, for God's sake tell him.'

'Shut up.'

Lomax lit a match.

'No!' screamed Naylor. 'No, please, no!'

'Who?' said Lomax. 'A name. Give me a name.' He held the match up in the air.

'No one! Myself. Only myself!'

Lomax sat still. As the match burned down to his fingers he blew it out, and dropped it on the floor. 'I want you to listen; listen really hard. Are you listening?' Lomax paused. 'I didn't hear you?'

'Yes. Yes, I am.'

'I know where you live, Naylor. I know all about you, Naylor. And I'll tell you this: if I ever see you again, hear you again, hear of you again, I'll be back, and I'll burn you. I'll burn you so hot and so much there won't be enough ashes left to fill an egg-cup. Understand?'

'Yes.'

'You sure about that, Naylor?'

'Yes.'

Lomax leaned back in the chair, and slowly tucked the matchbox back into his pocket. He put the revolver down on the floor, and walked a few paces towards the door. He took one more long drag on the cigar, then, suddenly, flung it on the bed and slammed the door shut behind him.

Naylor and his wife dived forward. Naylor flicked frantically at it, seized it by the lighted end, so that it burned his fingers. 'Owww, owww, owww!' he howled, rushing to the window, and hurling it out. 'My hand, my hand!' He jammed his fingers in his mouth.

'Why didn't it burn?' she said. 'Why didn't it?'

Naylor ran to the sink, turned on the cold tap, and put his hands under it.

His wife grabbed the top blanket and began to sniff. 'You berk,' she said. 'It wasn't petrol, wasn't any bloody petrol. He soaked us in water!' She began to cackle with laughter, hysterical with relief. 'My God, he made you look a berk.'

Naylor glared at her. 'You know why he used water?' he choked out, almost hysterical. 'Because he didn't have the fucking bottle.'

'You what?'

'Bottle. Didn't have what it takes. Not what I got.' He tapped his chest. 'Bottle. I got fucking bottle.'

'So I've heard.'

'I'll get him,' he said, 'I'll get that bastard.' He seized the revolver off the floor, and ran out, and down the stairs. He saw a light on in the kitchen and a shadow of movement. He walked down the passage.

Lomax looked up from behind the fridge door. He finished his drink of milk, put the bottle back and closed the door. He watched as Naylor raised the revolver and pulled the trigger. He watched him pull again, and again. He walked over to Naylor, grabbed the barrel of the gun, kicked away Naylor's shins, grabbed his throat, and rammed his head into the wall. 'You'd better get a hearing aid, Naylor,' he said, 'You obviously didn't hear me as well as you thought.'

He turned Naylor around. 'Know what's stopping me from taking you to the nearest rubbish tip and dumping you on it? I'll tell you: they recycle rubbish. I couldn't bear the thought of you being recycled, Naylor. When you go, you're going for good. And that'll be the next time we meet.' He reached an arm out past Naylor, to the fridge door. He opened the door a fraction, put his hand behind it, then yanked the door out, hard, crashing it against the back of Naylor's head. He allowed the dazed man to slip to the ground, and walked out of the kitchen, through the back door into the yard. This time he used the gate out into the twitten.

When he reached the road, he stopped by the kerb, pulled six .38 shells out of his pocket, and dropped them carefully down the drain. As he walked across to his car, he heard a motorcycle splutter into life behind him. He frowned. He was certain he had hit Naylor hard. Maybe the man was more resilient than he had realised. He looked over his shoulder and saw the beam of a light. 'Okay, my friend,' he said to himself, climbing into the car, and starting the engine.

Almost immediately, he saw the single light of the motorcycle pull out of the twitten behind him. Lomax accelerated up to the 30mph limit. The bike stayed behind him. He came to a red traffic light, and debated whether to jump it, or stop. He decided to stop. A short distance behind him, the motorcycle stopped.

The next lights were also red. Lomax stopped again, and Naylor halted behind him. A short distance further, and the speed limit ended. The road climbed up to the left, almost straight. Lomax floored the accelerator of the old but powerful car, and watched the speedometer climb past eighty, towards the ninety mark. The bike was right on his tail, no more than ten or fifteen feet behind. They hurtled through a wide left-hand bend, and the road straightened out again. He kept the pedal flat on the floor, and the needle slowly inched past the ninety mark. Lomax glanced once more into the mirror, to check Naylor's position, then took his feet off everything, and with all his strength, pulled on the handbrake.

He saw the light hurtle off to the right, heard the scream of tyres, saw the bike pass him on the outside, snaking ferociously. Suddenly, it turned sideways, flipped over, and began to somersault along the road, dragging Naylor with it. There was a tremendous dull bang, and then there was a clattering sound, like a wheel turning. A piece of metal rolled along the road in front of him, breaking the eerie silence that now suddenly dominated the night.

He restarted the stalled engine, and drove up the road. Naylor and his bike had come to rest in a bus shelter, partially demolishing it. It was not immediately possible to distinguish, from a first glance, which bits belonged to Naylor, which to his bike, and which to the Corporation of Northwich. He wound up his window, and accelerated away.

CHAPTER FOURTEEN

Andrea was sheet white when he arrived back at the hotel room. 'Where have you been?' she said, weakly. 'I was so frightened; so frightened.'

He lay down on the bed, and held her tightly. 'I'm sorry,' he said. 'You needn't be frightened anymore.'

'I didn't think you were coming back.'

'Of course I was coming back. Come on, dry your tears.'

'Big sodding romantic evening this is,' she said. 'On my own in a bloody four-poster bed.'

He nibbled her ear. 'We could make up for it now.'

She rolled away from him. 'Leave me alone.'

He lay back against the soft pillow, trying to think of something he could say. His thoughts went straight back to Naylor. Someone had put Naylor up to this. He wasn't smart enough to have thought it up on his own. Who? Who? He heard rhythmic breathing coming from Andrea. He looked over; she was asleep. He suddenly felt tired, dog tired, too tired even to undress, but his brain was whirring, madly. Who? He went over the names again: Stratton; Dean; Reynolds; Brabrook; Pember. The names echoed around in his mind. Pember. Pember. That name stuck out. Pember. Pember had been the oldest of the team. His last case before retirement. He had talked of moving up North. Wanted to buy a farm, a smallholding. Was he up here, somewhere? Was Pember behind Naylor? Had Pember taken the money? But if so, what did he want with Naylor? Why did he send a thug out to collect? Surely Pember knew it couldn't have been him. Was Pember just guessing? Was he testing everyone in turn? As the first light began to filter through the curtains, he fell into a deep but troubled sleep.

The click of a suitcase woke him, and he smelt a tang of scent. He opened his eyes, and saw Andrea, dressed, standing over the bed.

'Goodbye,' she said.

'Huh?'

'I'm off.'

She looked tired; strained; but still pretty. He liked her, something about her; the inner toughness; resilient; in spite of what she had been through, she had stayed composed. She had guts. He liked women with guts. It had been a long time since he'd met a woman he really liked. And now she was going. He put out his hand, and she took it, tenderly. He pulled her towards him, and she sat down beside him.

'Don't go.'

'Where did you go last night?'

'I had an appointment.'

'Business?'

'Sort of.'

'What kind of business are you in that you have appointments in the middle of the night? Burglary?'

Lomax grinned. 'No. I'm not a burglar.'

'Then what are you?'

He looked at her. 'I do odd jobs. I told you; a bit of this, bit of that.'

'Did you have a date?'

'I don't have that much energy,' he said.

'You didn't even get undressed last night.' She began to stroke his forehead, lightly, with her fingers. 'You know, Max, I came away – up here – looking for some excitement – break out of the mould before it was too late.' She shook her head, and smiled sadly. 'I'm not cut out for it. People setting fire to me; demanding money. Talking about guns, tooling-up, wasn't it?'

Lomax nodded.

'Midnight assignments. It's not me; none of it. Deep down, I'm just an ordinary housewife. That's what I was;

101

that's what I'd like to be again.'

'Rubbish.'

'It's true, Max. Cooking tea for the kids – fish fingers, baked beans, boiled eggs and soldiers. Comfortable house, nice little garden.'

'Dinner out on Saturday once a month. Conjugal rights afterwards, looking at the light fitting and thinking of England?'

She laughed. 'I'd prefer that to being cremated alive.'

'I'd call that being buried alive,' said Lomax.

She shrugged. 'You're a nice guy, Max. I like you, a lot; really I do. But you're not my scene; really you're not.'

They sat in silence for a moment; she continued to stroke his head. 'Are you in trouble, Max? Big trouble?'

'Not exactly.'

'In trouble with the law?'

'No.'

'With the Mafia?'

He smiled. 'Don't get too many Italians up here, round these canals. They prefer Venice.'

' You see. You're a closed book; evade everything. You promised to tell me everything, and you've told me nothing. Did you steal one hundred thousand pounds?'

'No.'

'Do you have one hundred thousand pounds?'

'I haven't counted lately.'

'That man thinks you do.'

'People can think what they like. One of the advantages of our society. Freedom of choice.'

'Yes, Max.' Her voice became softer. 'That's what I'm exercising now. My freedom of choice. Reluctantly, but definitely.' She leaned over, and gave him a final kiss on his forehead.

He lay back on the bed for a long while, in the empty room, then he heaved himself off the bed, splashed some water on his face, paid the bill and checked out.

He drove back to Hurst's boat-yard, stopping at

Sainsbury's on the way to stock up with provisions. He parked the car and hung the keys back on their hook in Hurst's office.

He was just about to lift the heavy box of groceries out of the boot of the car, when something caught his eye. He glanced sideways, wondering if he had been mistaken. But the movement of the bush convinced him he hadn't. He turned his attention back to the box, then threw a sideways glance again. The glint was unmistakable.

Furious, he sprinted out of the boat-yard, turned left, and down the lane. A figure ahead of him also broke out of the bush, a tall, thin man, young, quite different to the short Fleet Street hack of yesterday.

'Hey!' shouted Lomax. 'I want a word with you.'

Clutching his camera, the man vaulted over a wall into another boat-yard. Lomax followed. He saw the man ducking and weaving between a pile of boats, and then running around the back of a small factory. Lomax followed. For a moment he lost him. He looked wildly around, and then saw a figure disappear over another wall at the back. Lomax ran over to it. It was a high wall. He jumped up twice, but with no luck. He tried a third time, and managed to get a grip on the top. It was jagged with glass and cut his fingers. He heaved himself up, without caring, and dropped down the other side, landing on top of a dustbin and tumbling over with it.

He was in a passageway, and there was no sign of anyone, either to the right or left. He turned right, and ran for a hundred yards. He came out on to a communal tip; no sign of the man; no sign of anyone. He turned and sprinted back in the opposite direction, but he knew, already, he was too late. After three hundred yards, the passage ended at the towpath. He looked right and left. Nothing.

Fuming, he turned and walked back to the boat-yard. Hurst was in his office with a client. Lomax cursed; he wanted to use the phone, but did not want to be overheard. He walked back up to the village, and went into a call box.

'I'd like to make a reverse charge call to London,' he said.

"What number, caller?"

Lomax gave the operator the number.

'And what is the name of the party you wish to speak to?'

'Robinson,' he said. 'Mr Robinson.'

'And your name, please, caller.'

'Mr Goldfinger,' he said.

A minute and a half later, Robinson's quizzical voice was on the line. 'Robinson here?'

'It's Lomax.'

There was a brief silence the other end. 'Thanks for what you did yesterday, Max. You lost me my best photographer.'

'What a shame.'

'He quit on me.'

'Want me to weep?'

'Not on my paper's money, thank you.'

'Thought you learned your lesson a long time ago, Robinson. I'm a very private person. Don't like snoopers.'

'I was trying to protect you.'

'Kind of you, Robinson; didn't know you cared about my health.'

'I don't. I care about a good story. There's a better one in it for me if I keep you alive – long enough to lead me to the pot of gold.'

'What do you think I'm going to do? Go to the third tree on the left, turn right, walk fifty paces and start digging?'

Robinson grunted. 'Admire your taste in birds, Lomax. She's a nice one, that blonde. What's her name?'

'You don't know? You do surprise me.'

'He was a photographer, not a dick.'

'Well, you sure replaced him fast enough.'

'Replaced him? Are you joking? I can't work that fast. Anyhow, you made your point. You want to be left alone. OK, I'm leaving you alone; you're not the only game in town.'

'Doesn't seem that way from the trouble you take.'

'I'm busy, Max, and this call's expensive. Anything of interest you'd like to tell me?'

'Yes. Call off the new guy, or he'll be quitting on you too – if he's able to walk.'

'I told you. There isn't a new guy.'

'Are you serious?'

'Yes, I am.'

'Then how do you explain the photographer I've been chasing for the last half hour?'

'I don't operate every photographer in England, Max. Maybe it's the local rag. Want to see who else gets their fingers burned.'

'Very funny. Listen, Robinson; I've got a little tip-off for you.'

'Oh yes?'

'Myers Wharf, City of London docks. Know it?'

'I know the docks, Max.'

'You do travel to the best places, Robinson, don't you. There's a consignment of fridges being unloaded; in containers. Boat called *Samaran*. Make sure you've got someone there. Around eleven o'clock tonight. With a bullet-proof vest and plenty of film.'

'Is this a joke, Max?'

'I've still got a few friends in the Force.'

'Not what I hear.'

'Take it or leave it.'

'Nice of you to give me the choice.'

'More'n you ever gave me, Robinson.'

'What do you want me do? Send you a cheque for the tip?'

'No. Just a credit note.'

'Okay,' said Robinson. 'See you.'

'Not if I see you first.'

Lomax walked out of the booth, looking carefully around. Robinson was telling the truth for sure. He had sounded really sore. It took a lot to make a Fleet Street hack like Robinson sore. So who was the new David Bailey? He had run fast, he thought, been clever; knew how to escape; a pro. Too fast for the average booze-soaked newspaper photographer.

He walked back towards Hurst's yard, keeping a wary eye out. He was not happy with the way events were shaping; not happy at all.

CHAPTER FIFTEEN

Pember paced around the photographer's studio like a caged animal. He picked up a pile of eight by ten black and whites and leafed through them. 'Bit of an old slag this one, isn't she?'

The photographer looked icily at the tall, dark-haired man with the weak face and a beer gut in what was otherwise a trim frame. He didn't like people poking about amongst his things at the best of times. 'That's my wife,' he said.

Pember dropped the photographs back on the table with a loud bang. 'No offence,' he said. 'Just the angle of that particular photo – I mean the others – oh yeah, much better. Much better.'

The photographer closed the lid of the drier, and switched it on. 'Couple of minutes.'

'No hurry.' Pember picked up another pile. 'Blimey,' he said.

The photographer looked across, and nodded, blankly.

'Bit tasty, that one.' He pulled another out, and looked across at the photographer. 'You can go inside for things like this.'

'You the law or something?'

'No.' Pember laughed. 'No.' He picked up another pile. 'Gordon Bloody Bennett. How old's she?'

'Eighteen going on thirty-seven.'

'Now, how does a girl allow herself to do something like that?' said Pember.

'She gets drunk.'

'Oh yes?' He looked at it again, fascinated.

'Nice shot of the dog.'

'Oh yeah; beautiful. Eat your heart out, Barbara Woodhouse.'

There was a loud click, and the photographer opened the drier door. He stacked the prints together and put them in an envelope. 'There's your prints – and there's your contact sheets.'

Pember pulled out a wad of banknotes, and pulled off fifteen ten-pound notes. 'There's the other half.'

'Want a receipt?'

Pember held up the photographs, and grinned.

'What paper you work for?' said the photographer.

'Paper?' said Pember, momentarily forgetting his alias. 'Oh yeah. Freelance.'

'Features?'

'Features? Oh yeah; do a bit of features.'

'Who is he – this travelling man?'

Pember smiled. 'Come on, sunshine; you been snapping him for ten days; you tell me.'

'All I can tell you is he likes crumpet and runs fast.'

'Jogs?'

'Yes; jogs. And fucking sprints.'

'Sprints?'

'Caught wind of me the other day – day after he'd tumbled the Fleet Street merchant. I had a hell of a time losing him.'

Pember's face turned puce with rage. He grabbed the man by his tee-shirt, and pulled him tightly towards him. 'I told you not to get tumbled.'

'I – er, I didn't.'

'Did he see your face?' Pember's face was now an inch from his.

'No.'

'You sure about that?'

'Yes, yes!' he shouted.

'Did he follow you? Get your licence?'

'No!'

'He's a smart bugger. You sure?'

'Yes. I am sure.'

'If you're lying, my friend, you'll be sorry. Very sorry.' Pember released him, and the photographer stumbled backwards.

'You're not Press, are you, not Press at all.'

Pember turned in the doorway. 'You'd better keep your trap shut, my friend.' Pember pulled an imaginary zipper across his lips. 'If you want to stay healthy.'

'I want to see your Press Card.'

'You'll see it all right,' said Pember, 'if you mention this to anyone. Anyone. Straight between your eyes.'

The sweat poured down Lomax's back, as he bent down and picked up another crate of empties, in the back yard of the canal-side pub.

A few minutes earlier, a barge had slid by with a young boy on the helm. Lomax had rushed over to the towpath to get a closer look, certain that it was Steve. He had even called out, but when the kid turned, and waved cheerily, he had realised he was mistaken, and waved helplessly back.

If he could get to Steve, speak to him, maybe that was all that was needed. A friendly smile. 'It's all right, Steve. I'm not going to make you go to Canada. You can stay here. With me. Always.'

Lomax felt a sense of despair. Even if he did find him, what could he do? Jan had legal custody. The police would have been asked by Jan to keep a look out. From the reaction he had had from the police, certainly in London, they would have great pleasure in taking Steve, and arresting himself. How could he fight the legal system? The system that had given Jan custody of Steve, enabled her to go to court, get an order insisting that Steve, his son, should forcibly leave the one place he loved and the one parent he loved, and go to Canada, to her? If I could clear my name, he thought; clear my name, get a pardon, then I could go to court, fight that damned order.

For a moment, he felt a surge of optimism. But it drained away again, like the sweat on his back.

The sound of the sudden reversing of an old and noisy engine caught his attention, and he looked over his shoulder at the canal behind him. A grubby, rotting hulk of a narrowboat was being steered towards the bank by a wiry-looking youth, with a crew-cut and a red lumberjack shirt. Sitting on the cockpit rail, staring aimlessly at the water, was another youth with bright purple hair, and a young girl lay dozing on the cabin roof.

Lomax turned back to his crate, and stacked it on the pile. He felt a tremendous thump on his back, which sent him reeling forward. Behind him a thick Liverpudlian accent said: 'Oooh, sorry 'boot that.'

Lomax looked down at the mooring rope, which lay uncoiled around him, and silently bent down, picked it up, and walked over to the bollard. He gave it two turns around, and knotted it.

'Ta,' said the Liverpudlian, jumping ashore. 'Didn't mean t'hit'ya.' He paused. 'Is it openin' time?'

Lomax looked at his watch. He nodded.

'You workin' here?'

'I'm not doing this for fun.'

'Can we buy a couple of cases of beer – take away?'

Lomax led him through into the pub, and carried one of the cases out for him, to the boat. The purple-haired youth continued with his study of the water. Lomax hoped that Steve hadn't turned into a punk like him. The girl on the cabin roof sat up. She was a pretty freckle-faced girl, about fourteen or fifteen, he reckoned. She dangled her legs over the side, and smiled cheerily at him.

Lomax tugged the battered photograph of Steve out of his jeans pocket, and held it up to her. 'Ever seen him before?'

There was a gleam of recognition. 'Yes,' she said. 'I have.'

'You sure?'

'Yeah. His name's Simon – no – Steve?'

Lomax nodded, encouragingly.

'Other side of Chester.'

'How long ago?'

'Few weeks. You his dad?'

Lomax nodded. 'Did you talk to him?'

'No, not really; there was a group of us. I just remember noticing him, that's all.'

'What was he doing?'

'He was on a boat.'

'Do you know where he was heading?'

She shook her head. 'I'll ask around for you – there's a lot of kids down this way. Can I find you here anytime?'

'Mornings, 'til one, and evenings?' He nodded down the canal, to *Harmony*. '*Harmony*; that's my boat. If I'm not here, you'll always find me there. For a while, anyway.'

She smiled at him, a cheerful, almost impish smile. 'See what I can do.'

Lomax heard the engine start up, and jumped shore, just as the nose swung out, the stern still remaining attached to the bollard. He watched, as the scouse pushed the throttle harder forward, and the boat merely swung further out into the canal. He heard the pitch of the engine change to full revs, and a heavy wake began to slop against the bank.

'Hoy!' shouted Lomax. 'Hoy!'

The scouse looked over his shoulder. Lomax pointed at the rope. Immediately, he heard the sound of the engine being cut, and the scouse sheepishly looked round again. Lomax unwound the rope, coiled up his end, and hurled it at the scouse. The scouse completely missed the catch, it sailed over his head, and landed smack in the face of the spaced-out youth with bright purple hair.

She knew Steve's name, he thought, encouraged. So Steve was around here, somewhere. He would find him; he would. Quite what would happen when they did meet, he did not know; did not know what he even expected of his son. A big, tearful reunion? A cold, formal hallo, formal handshake, two minutes conversation, strangers on a railway platform, then the parting again, this time for ever? He had to know. Once he did know, it would be easier. Surely it would?

CHAPTER SIXTEEN

An hour later, when Lomax had finished stacking the crates, he went inside. It was only just gone noon, and already he could hear the general hubbub of conversation coming through the doors into the bars. He walked through the saloon entrance, hefted an empty barrel from the floor of the bar, and carried it out. Struggling under the weight, he carried a new barrel in. Hefting full barrels was his least favourite of pub work. They were always damned heavy, whatever their size.

He took a second empty out, and put it on the stack in the car park. He looked at his watch. He wasn't normally a clock watcher at work, but he felt tired this morning. He had been tired for the last couple of weeks, ever since Andrea had left him, in fact. The hurt had somehow got through to him; drained him. He wanted to go back to the boat now, and sleep. He heard a car pull into the car park, and idly looked around. A Ford Granada, with a single passenger in the back seat. It looked too smart to be a local taxi. The rear door opened, and a familiar bow-tied figure climbed out.

'Afternoon, Lomax,' said Robinson.

'Bloody hell,' said Lomax. 'Chauffeurs? You bastards really get the treatment, don't you.'

'You haven't seen anything yet, Lomax,' he smiled, then tapped on the driver's window, pointing his thumb to the boot.

The driver got out, and began walking around towards the rear of the car.

'All right, Robinson. How'd you find me? Eh?'

Robinson tapped the side of his nose, gently, and smiled an oily smile.

'You won't be able to do that much longer, Robinson.'

'Oh – why not?'

'Because one day I'm going to flatten it so much, won't be anything there to tap.'

Robinson looked pained.

'Anyhow, what brings you up here? Run out of news again?'

'I was wondering if you'd care to join me for lunch.' He looked round, and nodded towards his driver, who was struggling under the weight of a massive hamper.

'What the hell's that?'

'Lunch, Lomax.'

'Thought it was your laundry.'

'How about a picnic on your boat?'

'Very romantic. Just the two of us, with him as the wallflower.'

'I don't eat with the staff,' said Robinson, haughtily.

'Don't have an upstairs-downstairs on a narrowboat; unless he's brought a diving suit.'

'Take it,' said Robinson. 'It's for you.' He nodded, seriously.

Lomax held out his hands, and took the hamper. He sagged under the weight, and the driver smirked.

'What the hell's in here, Robinson? Your last wage packet?'

'How far's the boat?'

'You mean you don't know?'

Lomax stumbled the hundred yards to *Harmony*, and plonked the hamper down on the grass beside her. Then he lifted it again, and put it down in the cockpit of the boat. 'Jump aboard,' he said.

Robinson looked at the mooring hawsers. 'Enormous ropes,' he said.

'Good for bondage,' said Lomax.

'Really? I wouldn't know about that.'

'Expect voyeurism's more your scene, eh, Robinson?'

The reporter ignored the comment, and stepped on board, holding up his trousers carefully so as not to crease them. 'Never been on one of these before. Do I need Kwells?'

'Proper little Alan Whicker, aren't you? Last of the great explorers. I expect you consider taking the lift up to your office to be an adventure.'

'I was sick on the Serpentine once. By the way, I meant to ask – did you like that article I did? That welcome home piece? Not many cons get that, you know – only the really special ones.'

'Great, Robinson. Really great, don't do me any more favours like that, will you?'

'What's the matter?'

'Nothing. You just advertised my release to the whole world. Told every little Joe Schmuck who fancies his chance at a spot of blackmail that I've got a pot of gold. All they need do is find my missing son. Every day I wait for the ransom note to pop through the letter box.'

'Lomax. The serious ones – they don't need to read newspapers. They know what's what. Nothing I print is ever going to make a hill of beans of difference. It's only good old Joe Public reads newspapers; something to gobble down with the porridge, pass away the train journey.'

'Plenty of sickos in Joe Public.'

'Whole world's sick, Lomax; one of the facts of life. Fancy a drop of champagne?' Robinson flipped up the lid of the hamper. It was an Aladdin's cave of expensive bottles, tins and jars.

'Normal Fleet Street picnic?' said Lomax. 'Or do Fortnum and Mason owe you a favour?'

Robinson tugged out a pack of Bath Oliver biscuits, a jar of Beluga Caviare, and a knife. He pointed at a bottle of 1975 Krug. 'You buttle, and I'll wait,' he said, levering open the jar. 'You'll find some glasses in there somewhere. Cut glass, you know – none of your petrol station freebie jobs.'

Lomax poured the champagne, and handed Robinson a glass. Robinson passed him over a Bath Oliver with a half inch topping of caviare.

'Don't stint yourself, do you,' said Lomax.

'Never know where you are in Fleet Street,' said Robinson. 'One minute up, the next, down. My time could come tomorrow, next week, next year.' He shrugged and smiled. 'I'll just make sure that when it does come, I'm going to go down in style. Like the Titanic. Orchestra playing, corks popping.' He smiled his oily smile and took a greedy mouthful. While he chewed he held up his glass, and took a long swig of the golden yellow liquid; he swilled the mixture slowly around in his mouth, and then swallowed ecstatically.

'Good caviare this,' said Lomax.

'The best. I love it. I know it's fashionable to sneer. The rich man's yom kippur paté ... that's pure envy.' His voice suddenly became bitter. 'I used to know every lousy fish 'n' chip shop in Stoke on Trent. Know 'em and hate 'em. End of the week, you could wring vinegar out of my raincoat.' He took another long swig of his champagne.

'So,' said Lomax. 'To what do I owe the pleasure of a personal visit – thought I only rated your minions these days? And what is all this flash stuff, eh? Fortnum's hamper. Limmo. No bicycle clips?'

'A scoop, Lomax. Held the front page!' His voice turned bitter again, for a moment. 'The editor even remembered my name. Your City Docks tip. Remember?'

Lomax nodded.

'Came good.'

'Like I once told you, Robinson; you should listen to me more often.'

'Maybe I will.' He paused. 'Over a million quid's worth of hash, that raid, you know. One of the biggest ever. Did you see the front page? Going to clean up in the awards this year!' He took another swig of his champagne, and then another large mouthful of caviare and biscuit.

They ate in silence for a moment.

'Do you ever feel sorry for anyone?' said Lomax.

'Sorry?'

'Victims. Stuff you write about. That policeman, for instance, who was shot in that raid?'

'You've got to be detached; no emotion. Like the surgeon who only uncovers the bit he needs to work on. Man's inhumanity to man. Doesn't change, Lomax. Nothing changes, only the names, locations, and the excuses.' He dug his hand into the hamper, and pulled out a thick brown envelope. 'This is to say thank you for that tip.' He handed it to Lomax.

'What is it?'

'Your file. Clippings. The whole shooting match.'

'Why?'

'Because, finally, I believe you. You say you haven't the money. Okay. I believe it. Finis. Story's dead.'

'Was that second photographer last week yours?'

'No. He wasn't. Truth.' He tapped the package. 'It's all in there. Everything I have on you. Soup to nuts.'

'What's your game, Robinson?'

'No game. Far as I'm concerned, you're a free agent.' He paused. 'If, on the other hand –'

'Like conjuring,' said Lomax. 'There's always another hand, isn't there?'

Robinson smiled. 'If you ever want to pursue the "wronged cop" story, then that would tell very sweetly. Could get you a few grand for that, you know. I'll leave you my number. You can bell me, day or night.' He pulled out a card and handed it to Lomax.

Lomax studied it. 'Never associated you with a home.'

'Little igloo in Ealing; earth in the garden the colour of volcanic ash; tomatoes in the window boxes.'

'Don't remind me.'

'Flying ducks on the living room walls. A neighbour who practises the piano at six o'clock in the morning; one on the other side dying of lung cancer. And in 1997 it's all mine.' He paused. '"Vindictive police force punishes wrong man. Innocent does two years inside." It would be good, Lomax.'

Lomax smiled wryly. 'Six men on that caper. Only one went to the nick; the patsy; me. Did you ever try the other five?'

'One's retired. Pember. Two promoted. Stratton and

Brabrook.' He paused for a moment, thinking. 'One's transferred to the Fraud Squad – Thurley.'

'Wasn't really on the case,' said Lomax. 'Only about ten per cent of his time.' He paused. 'What about Dixie Dean?'

'London Airport. Anti-terrorist. That leaves –?'

'Willis,' said Lomax.

Robinson thought hard for a moment, and adjusted his bow tie. 'Willis. Coronary. The Met Convalescent Home at Hove.'

'Coronary? He wasn't that old. Christ. He was only forty-two.'

'Someone forgot to tell his heart that.'

'When did you last have tabs on Pember?'

Robinson held out another heaped Bath Oliver. 'Paté de foie gras? No moral objections?'

'If you're sick this afternoon, Robinson, don't blame the waves.'

Robinson smiled. 'A year. He's quite near here. Sold his house in Ruislip; bought an amusement park.'

'An amusement park?'

'Nothing fancy; not exactly Butlins. Carousel, couple of slides, dodgems that don't work. Boating lake with a few trout. Mum and the kids enjoy themselves whilst Dad goes fishing. Tacky joint, rather run down, in fact.'

'Where is it?'

Robinson thought hard for a moment. 'Daresbury,' he said. 'Just outside. Dale Park, Daresbury.' He paused. 'Yes, think that's it.' Robinson crammed the biscuit into his mouth.

'Any idea why he should think I have the money?'

Robinson smiled as he chewed, and began to spread paté on to another biscuit. 'Come on, Lomax. Everyone thinks you've got the money.'

'Except you?'

Robinson smiled again and said nothing.

CHAPTER SEVENTEEN

There was a muffled boom behind Pember, as a diamond-shaped monster from space exploded in a shower of green light. In another corner of the tatty pub, another electronic machine gave out an incessant blip-blop-blip-blop.

Pember lit a cigarette from the stump of a candle that was floating in water, on the table in front of him, whilst his eye remained fixed on the wiry, crew-cut scouse, in the red lumberjack shirt, who was locked in an arm-wrestling contest with one of the locals. A couple of other lads, one with purple hair, the other with his head shaven, egged the scouse on.

The scouse won the contest easily, and his mates roared with laughter. He got up, and walked past Pember to the gents. As he came back out, and walked past Pember, Pember called out. 'Kenny?'

The scouse stopped. 'How do you know my name?'

'Heard one of your mates call you.'

'Yeah. Kenny. That's me. King of the KOP.'

'An Everton fan!'

'Be the day!'

Pember pulled out his wallet, and inched a five-pound note out of it. 'See that?' He put his arm up into the traditional arm-wrestling position. 'Could be yours.'

'And if I lose?'

Pember pulled the candle out of the saucer, and stuck it firmly in the centre of the table. 'If you lose,' he said, smiling, 'you get burned.'

Kenny looked. 'Okay.' He sat down and put up his arm.

117

'Jees, you got a big bugger of a hand,' he said.

'Want to back out?'

Pember noticed Kenny's mates begin to drift over. 'Keegan man myself,' he said.

'Not fit to lace Dalglish's boots.'

They began their contest. Kenny exhausted himself, without succeeding in moving Pember's hand an inch.

'Like a fuggin' brick wall,' he grunted.

Slowly, Kenny's hand began to move backwards. Still he fought, until the hand was hovering just above the flame.

'Give in,' said Pember. 'Douse the candle.'

'I'm not fuggin' givin' in.'

The hand moved right down on to the flame. There was a crackle as the hairs burned off.

'How'd you like it done? Rare?'

The hand slipped further on to the flame.

'Give in?' said Pember.

'You getting squeamish?' said Kenny, the smell of burning flesh now in their nostrils.

'It'll burn you.'

''Tis burning me.'

Pember suddenly released his hand, and blew out the candle.

Kenny put his hand into his mouth, and began to suck. He looked tauntingly at Pember. 'Two sorts of strong,' he said. He pointed to Pember's arm. 'That one,' he said, and then tapped his own head. 'And that one.'

Pember tugged the fiver out of his wallet, and tucked it into Kenny's top pocket.

'Ta.' He began to stand up. Pember put a hand on his arm. 'Sore?'

'No. It's amazing what the sight of money does to me.'

'How'd you like another fifty of those?'

Kenny's eyes lit up. 'Wouldn't say no.'

Pember looked up, at the faces of Kenny's two mates.

Suddenly, Kenny understood. He looked up himself. 'Hey, I'm trying to talk a bit of business here. Why don't you all sod off?'

Pember waited until they were alone, then pulled a photograph out of his inside pocket. 'Ever see this man?'

Kenny looked at Lomax's face. 'Yeah; I have. Couple of days ago. 'Bout ten miles down the canal. Working in a pub. Yes, that were him.'

'Good,' said Pember. 'Very good.'

Lomax stood in the bar, wiping a glass. It had been hectic early on, now there was a bit of a lull. Lomax kept his eye on a Scot, in his late thirties, with heavily tattooed arms, wearing a grubby singlet, who had been loudmouthing for most of the evening, but was now slumped in a corner table, occasionally taking huge swigs from a pint mug, and allowing much of the beer to run down his face. The Scot suddenly emptied the remainder of his beer into the general direction of his face and stood up, unsteadily. He stumbled into the next table, stumbled back towards his own table, bumped into his own chair, and sat sharply down.

Then, suddenly, and determinedly, the Scot stood up again, and marched, slightly more steadily, towards the bar. He banged the glass down hard on the table, and tried to focus on Lomax's face. 'Another pint of yer muck, Jimmy.'

Lomax stared back at him.

'Have you got problems with your hearing?'

'I think you've had enough,' said Lomax, gently.

The Scotsman glared at him. 'Whatdyersay?'

'You heard.'

'You refusin' tae serve me?'

Lomax nodded.

'Sunshine, I'd drink you under the table any day.'

'I'm sure you could,' said Lomax, pleasantly. 'I'm not a drinker.'

The Scotsman banged his glass down hard, twice. 'Another pint, I'm telling you.'

'Tomorrow, eh? First pint's on the house.'

The Scotsman cocked his head sideways. 'How old d'ya think I am? Ten? Well, I'm not. I'm thirty-eight.' He tottered for a moment, then found his balance, and leaned forward, menacingly. 'Thirty-eight. Thirty-nine next birthday. I'll no' have anyone tellin' me when to stop drinkin'.' He raised his voice to a bellow. 'Now, give me another fuckin' pint!'

'Do yourself a favour, go home.'

The manager walked over, anxiously. 'Okay, Lomax?'

'Fine.'

'Want me to ring the nick?'

'No. Don't worry.' Lomax walked round to the front of the bar. 'Bedtime for you.'

The Scotsman took a wild swing at him, still holding the mug. Lomax slipped inside the punch, grabbed his arm, and whipped it up into a half-nelson. With his free hand, he eased the mug away, and put it on the counter. 'Nice and easy,' he said. 'Gently does it.' He propelled him outside. Two minutes later, he came back in, and went back behind the bar.

'All right?' said the manager.

'He just remembered – his mum said he had to be home by nine.'

The manager smiled. 'Thanks.' Then he looked at Lomax again. 'Done much fighting?'

'No. Can't stand the sight of blood. Especially my own.'

At ten to one the following afternoon, Lomax heaved out the last of the empty barrels. It was a scorching day, and he wiped away the sweat that was pouring down his brow and stinging his eyes. He went back into the pub. The landlord was standing in the store room, checking the stock list.

'Anything else you want me to do before I go?' said Lomax.

The landlord looked up at him. 'No, thanks. You have a good rest; goin' to be busy this evening, I feel.'

'Okay. Cheers.'

'Oh – by the way, Lomax – thanks for last night.'

Lomax shrugged.

'Could have been nasty. You handled it – er – very well.'

'Thanks. Wasn't anything.' Lomax nodded, walked back to *Harmony*, took a cold beer from the fridge, and sat down in the saloon, glad for a moment to be in the shade. He flicked over the pages of the morning paper. It was funny, he thought, how little news meant when he was on the water. In London, he couldn't live without newspapers. Here, although he bought a paper every morning, out of habit, he was never worried whether he read it or not.

'Anyone home?' said a gruff female voice that he vaguely recognised. 'Hallo?' said the voice, louder.

He stuck his head out of the cabin door. The scruffy-looking teenage girl he had seen the previous day, on the barge with the scouse, was standing on the bank. When she had been on the barge, he hadn't noticed quite how grubby she was. Torn jeans, filthy tee-shirt, and her golden hair matted with grease.

'Oh, hi!' she said, her cheeky freckled face lighting up. 'Couldn't remember if this was the right boat.'

In another couple of years, if she didn't go to fat, she'd be a stunner, thought Lomax. Right now, she was jailbait.

'Can I come aboard?'

'Help yourself.'

She hopped, childishly, both feet together, and nearly lost her balance as she landed.

'Hooligan!' said Lomax. 'You want to be piped, you should be dignified.'

'Aye aye, Captain.' She gave him a salute, hand flat against her forehead.

'That's an American naval salute. British sailors always have the flat of their hand parallel – like this.'

'Why?'

'Because they get shouted at if they don't.'

She stuck her head inside. 'Hey, this is pretty. Wow, it's beautiful. All that polished wood. Who polishes it?'

'The maid.'

'You've got servants?' She looked serious for a moment, then grinned. 'You're having me on!'

'Want a drink?' said Lomax. 'Coke or something?'

'I'll have a beer.'

Registering surprise on his face, Lomax went below, and

brought up a lager. He pulled the ring, and handed her the can. 'To what do I owe the honour of this visit?'

'Got some news. 'Bout your kid; not a lot of news.'

Lomax looked at her; wondered if she too had run away, whether there was some distraught parent roaming the canals in search of her. 'Any's better than none,' he said.

'He was working for a firm in Chester. Glendinnings. They own three or four boats. Steve told one of the girls he'd been there for some weeks, but was moving on. Said he might go down the Llangollen – or else up the Leeds and Liverpool.'

'That's two opposite directions.'

She nodded. 'I said it wasn't a lot of news. Girl he spoke to got the impression he was hiding from someone.'

'Hiding?'

She nodded. 'Does he know you're looking for him?'

'I would have thought so, by now. I don't know. Maybe not. Canal's a big place. Anything else?'

'Not really.'

'Thanks for your trouble.'

'No sweat.'

'Can I offer you a bite of lunch? I was about to have a tuna sandwich?'

'Thanks. I'm starving.' She put her head inside the cabin again, and looked around. 'Couldn't ask you a favour, could I?'

'You can always ask.'

'Have you got a shower?'

He nodded.

'Mind if I use it?'

'Sure. Reckon you'll enjoy your sandwich more?'

'No. You will. My hair's filthy; haven't had a shower since – lumme, I can't remember.'

'You up here on holiday?'

'Live here,' she said. 'With my fella; on that barge you saw yesterday.'

'You live on that?'

She nodded, and smiled. '*Paradise*.'

'Paradise?' said Lomax.

'That's its name!'

'Highly appropriate,' said Lomax, dubiously. 'How old are you?'

'Don't get nosey,' she said. 'Where's the soap?'

'In the fridge.'

'Fridge?' She looked puzzled, then a grin broke out on her face. She jumped down through the hatch. Lomax followed.

'I'll get you a towel,' he said.

'And a sheet of sandpaper.'

'Don't rub too hard. Your freckles might come off. I'll go and make a picnic on the bank.'

Half an hour later, they sat in the grass by the boat, swigging back the last drops of their lagers. Susie tossed her wet hair back from her face. 'So you haven't seen him for two years?'

'No.'

'Where were you?'

'Abroad. On business.'

'Sad,' she said.

'Yes,' he said. 'I am.'

'I was thinking of him.'

'Kids today are resilient,' said Lomax. 'Look at yourself.'

'Resilient?' she said.

'You don't agree?'

'One of those words parents use. Always trot it out when couples are splitting up.'

Lomax smiled, guiltily.

'You think anyone ever stops to ask them, "Hey, Tiny Tim: your mum's movin' another fellah in; your house is up for sale and you're changing schools again. But you're a resilient kid, aren't you?"'

Lomax looked at her, and nodded his head, slowly. 'You're smart,' he said.

'I read a lot,' she said, flatly. She drained her beer can, then ran a finger through her hair.

'Feel better?'

'Feels like hair.' She smiled. 'Mr Lomax, you're a lucky guy.'

'How's that?'

'I'm going to do the washing up.'

'That's kind of you – but there's only two plates.'

'That's why I'm offering,' she said, scooping up his plate. 'I'm not stupid, you know.'

She stood up, and grinned as he laughed. 'You want a coffee?'

'Black; no sugar.'

'Be right back.'

Lomax lay back in the grass, watching idly as she walked through the saloon, and into the galley.

An hour later, Susie walked across a wide field, and up towards a helicopter that was parked outside a huge barn. There was a smell of aviation fire and the rattle of a diesel generator grew louder as she approached. Kenny, stripped to the waist, was holding a nozzle attached to a long rubber tube, against the side of the helicopter. The tube ran back and into the barn. Behind him, two men were unloading sacks off a lorry in the barn.

'Hi,' he shouted at her. 'How'd it go?'

'He's nice,' she said.

'That's not what I asked,' said Kenny, irritated.

'Went like clockwork.'

'What did you do with it?'

She looked at him, hesitating for a moment. Then she spoke, almost reluctantly. 'There's a jamjar in the galley; on the window sill. Full of pencils, pens. I put it in that.'

'It safe? Not going to fall over?'

She shrugged. 'Seemed a good place.'

'He wasn't suspicious?'

'Why should he be?' She paused and looked up at the helicopter. 'Wish you'd learn to fly that, you could take me up.'

'You sure he wasn't suspicious?'

'Course he wasn't. Would Doug take me up?'

'How do you know he wasn't suspicious?' he said, irritably.

'If you haven't got confidence in me, then don't ask me to do the job.'

'All right; only asking. There's money at stake.'

'Good as in the bank.'

'You look different. What you done?'

'Washed my hair. I used his shower.'

Kenny nodded, then suddenly looked worried. 'Where was he?'

'Scrubbing my back,' she said, standing well back, with a taunting expression on her face.

CHAPTER EIGHTEEN

Lomax stood in the call box. 'I'll have to hang up when the pips go, Karen. Haven't any more ten pees. She doesn't sound too good, does she?'

'She's tough,' his sister said, but her voice lacked any conviction.

'Isn't there anything else the doctor can do?'

'She's got to have rest. Physiotherapy. Says time's the only thing.'

'How about getting a second opinion?'

'I'll have a word with Dad.'

The pips went. 'Call you in a couple of days,' he said, and hung up.

He walked out of the booth, picked up his box of groceries, and headed back down to the towpath. His mother was slipping away. It was clear. And she would die without ever knowing the truth.

He heard a car as he reached *Harmony*, and looked round. An unmarked police Montego pulled up behind him, and two plainclothes detectives climbed out. One, senior looking, thick set with a broken nose. The other in his mid-twenties, with a mean face; a rookie, he thought.

The senior one flashed his card. Detective Inspector Jakeman, C.I.D, he read. The two men stared provocatively at him.

'This your barge?' said Jakeman.

'Narrowboat,' said Lomax.

'Got a name?'

'*Harmony*,' he said.

Jakeman looked at him for a moment. 'Your name,

sunshine,' he said, humourlessly.

'Lomax. Max to my friends.'

'Lomax, eh?' He turned to the junior. 'Lomax, eh? Max to his friends, eh? Rings a bell to me; ring a bell to you?'

'Yeah,' said Greasely. 'That does ring a bell.'

'Sort of warning bell,' said Jakeman. 'Name Susie Keswick ring a bell to you, Lomax?' he said.

'What about her?' said Lomax.

'You know her?'

'No.'

Jakeman feigned surprise. 'That's not what I hear. That what you hear, Doug?'

'No. Not what I hear.'

'Not what either of us hear,' said Jakeman. 'Little dickie bird told me you two had a cosy lunch together. Very cosy.'

'Had lunch with a Susie, yes. Didn't know her name was Keswick.'

'So many are there – don't bother with names, that it?'

'Some law says I have to know names?'

'There's laws about interfering with minors, Lomax. Thought you might know that; man of your experience.'

'If you're worried about her moral welfare, I suggest you go and talk to her boyfriend. The one she lives with.'

Jakeman cleaned out the inside of his mouth with his tongue. 'Missing from home. Her father would like her back. Intact, Lomax.'

'You can re-tread tyres. Virginity's a bit harder.'

Jakeman looked him up and down. 'Mind if we have a peep round your – er – yacht? Bit of a sailing man myself. Both are, come to think of it – isn't that right, Detective Constable Greasely?'

Greasely nodded.

'You got a warrant?'

'Just a friendly peep. Know what I mean?' said Jakeman.

'As it's friendly, just one of you.'

'Oh – why's that?'

'That way I can watch. Easier to watch only one.'

'Suspicious?' said Jakeman. 'Nervous, eh?'

'Hate you to find something... like something you brought with you.'

'If I were you, I wouldn't go round making that sort of allegation. Very dodgy.'

'I'll show you around,' said Lomax. 'The gorilla stays on shore.' He smiled cheerfully at Greasely, who scowled back, and shoved his box of groceries into Jakeman's hands. 'Give me a hand, thanks.' He jumped on board, and Jakeman reluctantly passed him the box, then followed him on board.

'Where would you like to start?' he said. 'There's above deck or below deck. This is above deck.'

Jakeman nodded towards the hatch, and Lomax led him through.

'Very cosy,' said the inspector, looking around. He studied the drinks cabinet. 'Vodka, rum, ten-year-old single malt. Soften 'em up first, do you? Live like a king, don't you. Still, word is you can afford to.'

'Like a drink?' said Lomax.

'Proper little floating pimpmobile this,' said Jakeman, ignoring the offer. 'Should think you get plenty, with this little set up.'

'Like a regular bunny rabbit,' said Lomax.

Jakeman eyed the budgerigar. 'Does he talk?'

'If you torture him first.'

Jakeman ignored the barb, and ran his eyes around the galley. He pulled open a cupboard, and looked in, sniffing. 'Health foods, eh? Plenty of bran. Bit of a food faddist, are you?'

'I like to keep regular,' said Lomax, following him through to the bedroom.

Jakeman tested the bed. 'Bit hard. Ideal for your purposes; tiring if the bed's too soft.'

'Is it?'

Jakeman turned to face him. 'My Super... little fat guy with round glasses, egg bald, to look at him, you'd think butter wouldn't melt in his mouth.' He leaned forward, put his face close to Lomax. 'He can get blood out of a crowbar, he can.'

'With a trick like that, he should be on the stage.'

Jakeman stared silently at him for a moment, then walked back to the galley. He lifted the lid of a pot, and sniffed the cold stew.

'Hungry?' said Lomax.

Jakeman ignored him. He opened and shut a couple more cupboard doors, then his hand reached the jamjar full of pencils and pens. He lifted it up, slowly, toyed with it, playing, turned it around. Then, suddenly, and violently, he turned it upside down and shook the contents out on to the work surface. He stared at the pens, the pencils, an india-rubber, a pair of compasses, held the jar up, looking care-fully inside to make sure nothing was stuck there, turned it up again, then stared Lomax in the face.

Lomax stared him straight back, expressionless, except for the minutest trace of a smile on his lips.

Jakeman put the jar down, gently. 'If I said "pot" – what would you think of?'

Lomax pursed his lips, and scratched the back of his neck, distinctly aware that, for the moment, at any rate, he had the upper hand. 'Chickens,' he said.

'Chickens?'

Lomax nodded.

'Why?'

'It's what Roosevelt promised Americans – chicken in every pot.'

Jakeman stared at him, for a long time, in silence. 'Want some free advice, Lomax?'

'I was always taught that if something was free, it couldn't be worth having.'

'If I were you, I'd move on.'

'Would you?'

'Failing that, I'd be awful careful.'

'Lot of slippery steps?'

'Like glass.'

'Particularly under-age girls?'

'Nothing in particular; nothing specific. Anything, Lomax; anything at all. If I saw you look at runner beans on an allotment, I'd nick you for intent.'

'Can't say fairer than that.'

'You're catching on, Lomax.' Jakeman gave Lomax a short, hard smile, then spun on his heels, and walked out through the saloon.

The ripple died away, and the fly began to sink through the calm water. Pember drew the rod back, gently at first, then sharply, and then flicked it forward. The line snaked out over the lake behind him, the fly trailing on its cast behind that, then the line curled forward, until it was straight out in front of him. Slowly, gently, it dropped down on to the water. The fly hovered on the end of its cast, and finally dropped, once again making a light ripple.

Out of the corner of his eye, Pember saw a silver Montego come slowly down the drive of the empty amusement park, past the carousel and the dodgems, and pull up at the edge of the lake. The burly figure of Jakeman climbed out. Pember wound in the line, and rowed the punt to the shore.

'Anything biting?' said Jakeman.

'Too hot,' said Pember. 'Sun's too bright.'

'Always an excuse, eh? You fishermen. Sun's too bright, not enough sun. Lake's too high, lake's too low. You should take up clays.' He raised his arms, and pretended to shoot down a clay-pigeon. 'Predictable sport. Only one thing to blame if you don't hit 'em. Yourself.'

Pember smiled. 'How's the big fish?'

'Sun's too bright,' said Jakeman. 'Water too low.'

Pember looked worried. 'What's that meant to mean?'

Jakeman shook his head. 'Wasn't there.'

'Wasn't there?'

Jakeman shook his head. 'Went along yesterday. Bare as Mother Hubbard's cupboard. Tipped the jar up; nothing.'

'You got the wrong jar.'

'Bollocks.'

Pember spat on to the ground. 'He's a clever bloody sod.'

'Yeah.'

'What about the girl? Screwing a minor?'

Jakeman shrugged. 'He knows the ropes.'

'You threaten to lean on him?'

Jakeman nodded. 'Didn't exactly wet himself.'

'Maybe you ought to lean on him a bit harder; put the frighteners on.'

'He won't frighten easy.'

'I wasn't suggesting we made it easy.' He looked down at the water for a moment. 'I don't want him turning up here. I want him shifted; further the better. I want him to get the message loud and clear.'

'We can keep an eye on him,' said Jakeman. 'Wait for him to put a foot wrong.'

'And if he doesn't?'

'Difficult.'

'Come on, you know the routine. You can make life unpleasant. He's got a job, hasn't he?'

Jakeman nodded. 'The Anchor. Barman.'

'Don't reckon he's got much dough. Needs to work, needs to go where the work is. Harder for him to come snooping if he's fifty miles away. Get the message?'

Jakeman nodded. 'We'll try.'

'Yeah,' said Pember. 'Why don't you try? Real hard.'

An hour later, Pember walked up to Kenny's barge. 'Anyone home?' he shouted.

A moment later, Kenny's crew-cut head peered out of the hatch. 'Afternoon,' he said.

Pember looked disdainfully at him then looked at the boat. 'Ever heard of a paintbrush?' he said.

'Paint costs money.'

'So does not doing your bloody job,' said Pember.

'Oh yeah?'

'There wasn't anything. In the fucking jar. Nothing. What's the game?'

Kenny looked worried for a moment. 'It was there. She put it there.'

'You sure?'

'Course I'm bloody sure.'

131

Pember stared at him. 'Well, it didn't bloody work.'

Kenny shrugged. 'I was paid to deliver. I delivered.'

'Don't reckon I've had my money's-worth,' said Pember.

Kenny shrugged. 'Next time I deliver anything for you, I'll get a receipt.'

Pember stared at him in silence. The scouse stared back, unyielding. Pember turned, looked around, then faced the scouse again: 'I want you to make life unpleasant for him. Very unpleasant; know what I mean?'

'Shouldn't be difficult,' said Kenny. 'For the right kind of money. Know what I mean?' he said, emphatically, staring Pember straight in the eye, and rubbing his finger and thumb together.

CHAPTER NINETEEN

The last of the evening's drinkers tottered out of the pub. Lomax closed the door, thankfully, and locked it. He scooped a handful of tumblers off a table, and carried them to the bar.

'You were right,' he said to the landlord. 'Was a busy evening.'

'Aye. Thursdays. Hot on a morning, Thursdays, they come out like flies in the evening.'

Lomax took the glasses behind the counter, and turned the tap on.

The landlord came up and stood beside him. 'Bit of an embarrassing situation's come up,' he said, in an uncomfortable, stilted, voice.

Lomax looked at him.

'Edna... one of my regular girls... left to have a baby. Didn't imagine I'd see her back much before the end of the summer – well – she dropped in tonight, you see. Money at home's tight. Husband on the dole.' He paused, and went red in the face. 'To cut it short, she'd like her job back.'

'My job?' said Lomax.

'If I don't take her, she going to take a job in that Cohen's factory; blouses or summat, they make. She's a good girl, pretty, got the gab. Need dolly birds in here in winter, you know, pulls the lads.'

'I never did look too good in a frock,' said Lomax, bitterly.

'I am sorry about it. Unfortunate situation. Hope you understand?'

'Understand. Oh, sure, sure I understand.'

'No sense being unreasonable.'

Lomax looked at him. 'Don't piss about with your excuses. Don't tell me bloody lies.'

The landlord looked at the ground, and looked up again at him. 'I'm sorry, Lomax; but I've a business to run. My pub this. Heavy mortgage.'

'Everyone's got a heavy mortgage.'

'Aye.' He nodded slowly. 'Don't worry about those glasses. I'll do 'em. I'm sorry. Really I am.' He dug his hand into his pocket. 'Look – I owe you thirty-eight. I've rounded it up to fifty. Fair?' He handed the wad to Lomax.

Lomax looked down at the money, and peeled off twelve pounds. 'Spent a night in Singapore, once. After the meal – marvellous Cantonese grub – I went to tip the waiter. He refused. I asked him why. Know what he said?'

The landlord shook his head.

'We don't accept tips,' he said. 'It's too demeaning.' Lomax stuffed the notes into the landlord's shirt pocket, and walked out of the pub.

Fuming with rage, he walked across the car park and on to the tow-path. Then he stopped in his tracks. There was no sign of his boat.

He ran up to the mooring bollards, and stared out at the black water. Somewhere in the dark night, he thought he heard a titter of laughter, but it stopped as abruptly as it had started. His face flushed. Perhaps she had slipped her moorings? Impossible; there was no wind and no current. He looked up to his left, where there was a long, straight patch of water, partially illuminated by the street lamps on the road that ran parallel; nothing. To his right, the canal curved away, out of sight.

He turned right, and began to run.

After half a mile, as he rounded another curve, he saw a dark shape, on the far side of the canal, sticking out of an overhanging tree. He stared, intently. It was *Harmony*. He breathed a sigh of relief, then he remembered, there was no bridge for a good mile in either direction.

He wedged his money tightly into his pocket, and then

dropped himself into the water. His feet sank into the slimy mud, and pulling them out, the suction almost removed his shoes. He knelt down, and began to swim.

Someone had deliberately tried to hide the boat; there was no way she could have drifted this far into the bushes. He started her up, reversed out, and then cruised back up the river, to where he had moored before. This time, he took two long ropes, making several turns around each of the bollards, then brought the ropes back on to the boat and made them fast on the far side of the deck. If anyone wanted to set him loose during the night again, they would have to either cut the thick hawsers, no easy job, or else board the boat to get to the knots.

He went down below, showered off the dirty canal water, and then lay down on his bunk. He thought about the girl, the visit from Jakeman, the nervous face of the landlord. Maybe he was being too passive, he thought; perhaps he should start to hit out, hit hard. But where? How? What with? And, most important, who? Someone sent a spiv to collect the money. Someone hired a young girl to frame him. The police put the frighteners on a pub landlord. Someone untied his boat. He smiled, sadly. Peace. That was why he first was drawn to the canals. On the canals you could be anonymous, a water gypsy, free of everything. He had thought they would leave him alone, up here. But no. Would they ever leave him alone? Anywhere? What did he have to do to get them to do that? Whoever they were. Change his name? Have plastic surgery?

Keep a grip, he told himself. Don't get deluded. You didn't do it. Innocent. You shouldn't be the one who has to run away; hide. You've got to find out who did do it; prove it; nail them. There's no other way at all.

The crash of drums nearly split his head open. He sat up, shaking his head in disbelief. The drums erupted into the even louder strumming of an electric bass guitar, followed by the piercing wail of an amplifier. He looked at his watch. It was a quarter to two in the morning.

He peered out of the window. A barge was moored next to

135

him, ablaze with light.

Lomax pulled on his dressing gown, and went up on deck. He recognised Kenny's hulk, immediately. The noise was bursting out of its cabin.

He jumped on to the embankment, walked around, and boarded the boat. He stuck his head in through the door. Kenny, whom he recognised, the purple-haired youth, whom he also recognised, a spiky-orange-haired youth, and a fourth youth, were sitting, with an array of musical instruments wired to an amplifier and two enormous speakers, frantically playing a tuneless cacophony. There was no sign of Susie.

'Hey!' shouted Lomax. 'Hey!'

The noise abated, and they looked up at him, four irritated faces.

'Know what time it is?' he said.

'No,' said the purple-haired one. 'Do you?'

For some reason Lomax could not fathom, they found this excruciatingly funny, slapping their sides hysterically with laughter. Lomax waited patiently for them to quieten down. 'Look, I'm trying to sleep,' he said.

'Finding it difficult without a fourteen-year-old to keep you company?' said Kenny, bitterly.

Lomax gave him a long look. He tried to think of some reply, but he was too tired. 'Think you could turn the noise down, just a bit?'

'It's loud music, mister,' said the spiky-haired youth.

'I understand that,' said Lomax. 'Does it need to be that loud?'

Kenny scratched his head, in feigned thoughtfulness. 'Yeah; yeah, I'd say it would. What you say, George?'

'Oh definitely,' said the youth with the purple hair. 'You see, mister, loud music don't sound right, less it's loud.'

Again they all burst into hysterical laughter.

'How much longer are you playing for?' said Lomax.

'We're practising,' said Kenny. 'Practising till we get good. Could take about ten years, I reckon.'

'Tell you what, mister,' said the spiky-haired youth. 'You

don't like it, why don't you push off?'

'Don't suppose there's much point in mentioning that I was here first?'

Kenny looked at him, and spoke gently, mockingly courteous. 'No, no good at all. Interesting of you to tell us, but no, awfully sorry. Important gig tomorrow, got to practise; got to get the right acoustics, you see. It's too bad you picked this mooring for a night's sleep. Famed for its acoustics, this mooring, You see. Best acoustics on the canal.'

'Really?' said Lomax. 'That's well worth knowing.' He returned to *Harmony*, and wearily began to untie the mooring ropes.

At half past seven the next morning, Lomax chugged slowly back down the canal, with a smile on his tired face. He reversed the engines as he came up to where the hulk was moored, and held *Harmony* stationary in mid-canal. All was quiet on the hulk, and it rocked gently in the wake he had caused.

Slowly, he eased *Harmony* in closer, until the two stereo speakers he had placed up on the roof were either side of the hulk's stern. Then he went through into the saloon, and hit the switch on the amplifier.

For a moment, the speakers sounded as if they were going to tear under the strain. Then *Eine Kleine Nachtmusik* erupted out into the still morning. He turned the volume control up still higher, then walked back up on deck, and casually leaned back against the rail.

The first sign of life appeared after about thirty seconds; a purple shock of hair atop a white face with red eyes peered, stupefied, out of the rear hatch. The head swivelled a few times, unable to grasp the situation, frowning and blinking simultaneously. A pair of fingers appeared, attached to a pair of hands, and found their way to its ears. His face screwed up in pain.

A second white face appeared, this one with a crew cut, and peered out.

Lomax smiled and waved cheerily.

Kenny heaved himself out of the hatch, and stood, stooped and blinking. He squeezed his temples, then put his fingers in his ears, and glared across at *Harmony*. He looked at each speaker in turn, and then Lomax.

Lomax went below, and switched off the amplifier; then he came back out. He watched Kenny slowly remove his hands from his ears, then he nodded slowly at the youth, and gave a broad grin. 'Morning!' said Lomax. 'Just thought I'd drop by and tell you were right about the acoustics. They really are terrific.'

CHAPTER TWENTY

Lomax stood in the chandlers, waiting for the elderly owner to finish an interminable phone call. Finally the man put down the receiver and nodded at Lomax.

'Do you have any mooring chain?'

'Chain?'

'Yes. I want two lengths of a hundred feet.'

'Got nylon rope.'

Lomax shook his head. 'No, I want chain.'

'Nylon's as tough. Much lighter.'

'No good. It can be cut.'

'Can cut chain too.'

'Not quite as easily.' Out of the corner of his eye, Lomax saw a young girl, carrying a package of groceries, standing at a bus stop.

'Haven't had any call for chain. Not for a long time.'

'Could you get some?' He saw a bus arriving.

'Could make a phone call.'

'Don't worry.' Lomax walked out of the shop, just as Susie was boarding the bus. He ran over, and jumped on behind her. She walked up the stairs, and down to the front of the bus. There was no one else up there. Lomax sat down beside her. She looked around at him, and jumped in shock.

'Morning,' he smiled.

'Good morning,' she said, nervously.

'Fares please,' said a voice.

'Thirty pence,' she said.

'Same,' said Lomax, handing the money. He took the two tickets, and the conductor went back downstairs.

139

'Where – where you going?' she said.

'Nowhere special,' said Lomax.

'I – er, I have to get off the next stop.'

'Can go further than that for thirty pence,' said Lomax. 'Relax, enjoy the view.'

'Thought you only travelled by boat?'

'Life's full of surprises, Susie,' said Lomax. 'You learn that as you grow older.'

'What do you want?'

'You left something behind on my boat. Rather careless. Thought you might need it back.'

She looked at him, her normally chirpy face nervous.

Lomax pulled a small dark brown square of cannabis out of his pocket, and held it up. 'Looks like chocolate.' He took a long sniff. 'Doesn't smell like it, though. Moroccan Gold, I'd say. Good stuff; quality.'

Susie tried to get up. Lomax pushed her back down on to her seat. 'We're going to have a chat, you and I.'

'Got people waiting for me.'

'Drop them a postcard.'

'I'll scream.'

'Scream. Go on.'

She stared ahead, sulkily.

'Shouldn't be careless with stuff like this; expensive. Could land yourself in a lot of trouble; or someone else.' He looked hard at her, and she went bright red.

'It's only pot,' she said, sullenly.

'You went to a lot of effort to lose it on my boat. Why?'

'I was nervous. Thought the law was on to me.'

'Try again.'

'It's the truth.'

'Come on, girl, I wasn't born yesterday. Someone put you up to this, someone who wants to get me into trouble. Who?'

'No one.'

'You drop by my boat, plop this in a jamjar, and next thing, the Old Bill poles up. What have I done to you?'

She continued to stare ahead.

'I could have gone inside for this. I haven't done you any

harm. Haven't done anyone around here any harm.'

'I have to get off.'

'You aren't getting off until you tell me,' he said, menacingly.

'I'm in no hurry,' she said.

'Thought you said you had people waiting for you.' He paused, and looked out of the window. 'Hear your dad's looking for you. Anxious about you.'

'What if he is?'

'Told him I'd bring you back.'

She looked at him, and suddenly went white. 'You wouldn't do that.'

'Wouldn't I? Found that kid I was looking for; returned him to his Dad. Kid wasn't happy about that, not happy at all.'

'But – you – that was your kid.' She stopped and stared out the window. 'You bastard,' she said. 'Wasn't your kid at all. Someone paid you to find him.'

Lomax nodded. 'My job. I find things for people. Kids, mostly, who've run away to the canals. Fifteen I've found and returned so far this year.' He looked at her again. She was trembling and her eyes were wet.

'Please,' she whispered. 'Don't take me back. I couldn't bear that.'

'Why not'

'I'm happy here. Please. I'm so happy here.'

'Not my problem. Got my job to do, you see.'

'If I tell you, will you let me go? Tell him you haven't seen me?'

'Why should I do that?'

'Please. He's a bastard. Beats me all the time.'

'I'm not surprised, you go around smoking that stuff.'

She shook her head. 'Wants to sleep with me. Beats me if I won't sleep with him. Gets terrible drunk. Please, don't make me. Please.'

'Who told you to plant the dope?'

'Kenny.'

'Kenny?'

'You know him. Crew cut; checked shirt.'

'Your fellow?'

She nodded.

'Now why would he do a thing like that?'

'I don't know,' she sobbed. 'Told me to do it. Told me I had to do it.'

'What does he do, this Kenny? Musician?'

'Wants to be. Works in the day time. Anderson's farm.'

'That where I'd find him today?'

She looked up at the sky. 'Clear today. Might be there. Might be up flying. You'd find him this evening; playing a gig up the road. The Welldiggers.'

Lomax stood up and opened the window. He hurled the lump of cannabis out, into the hedgerow.

'Hey!' she said. 'Hey! That was good stuff!'

'Smoking's bad for you,' said Lomax. 'Stunts your growth.'

'Don't smoke it. I eat it.'

'Stick to Mars Bars. They're better for little girls,' said Lomax, peering out of the window again. 'This is my stop coming up.'

An hour later, Lomax boarded *Harmony*, started the engine, and cast off, heading in the direction of The Welldiggers. He gave a wide berth to a long barge, low in the water under a heavy load of timber, that was travelling too fast, and planted his feet firmly on the ground as *Harmony* hit its bow-wave and pitched sharply. He heard the crash of a plate or a glass from the galley, and cursed the lumber barge.

A cabin cruiser approached, also travelling much too fast, a fat man in khaki shorts at the helm, and a fat woman in a muslin frock, legs dangling over the side of the cabin roof, waved cheerily. Lomax glared back by way of reply. He passed a couple of anglers, floats bobbing violently as the waves from the cabin cruiser crashed into the bank. They rounded a curve, and then the canal ran dead straight and empty in front of him, through a series of fields. He clamped the tiller, and hurried below, to grab a beer, then he came back on deck, opened it, laying the ring pull carefully down. Other people used the canals as rubbish tips, and it always upset him.

He sat down, and turned events over in his mind. The landlord's face in the pub; frightened; someone had leaned on him. Was the vendetta of the police really nationwide? What did a couple of detectives from a small provincial town really want to bust him for? To frighten him? Make him move on? Why? He could understand the attitude of the London police, where he had worked, where he had been known. A lot of bad odour there. But police forces in Britain didn't communicate with each other that much, didn't exchange much dialogue. Not unless there was a reason. No, someone had leaned on them, someone with influence up here. Could it be Pember? A retired London cop? What influence did he have up here? How could he have influence up here? But if not Pember, then who?

Somewhere in the back of his mind, he heard a clatter. Kenny, he thought; a crew-cut lout; what did he have to gain by planting hash on *Harmony*? It didn't make sense. The clattering became louder, and suddenly, he felt a smattering of rain. Puzzled, he put his hand up, as the rain became harder. Clear blue sky? What the hell? Everything was going mad.

Suddenly he was in the midst of a howling, lashing vortex. The rain was bright orange, and it burned his eyes, stank, stuck to him. Shielding his eyes, he tried to look up, could see nothing, the clattering was deafening. And then he realised.

He dived below, slamming shut the door, whilst the orange chemical pounded down, drumming on the roof, the deck, sliding in rivulets down the windows.

The engine! he suddenly thought. There was no way of switching off the engine, nor steering from here. In a minute, the boat would inevitably hit one side of the embankment or the other, or, worse, something coming the other way. 'Bastard,' he said, quietly. 'Bastard.' He grabbed his oilskin, pulled it on, pulled the hood over his sticky hair, took a deep breath, flung open the door, and jumped out into the torrent.

He switched off the engine, and grabbed the tiller. It wouldn't move. Still clamped, he remembered. He swung off the clamp, pushing the tiller hard over, as the bank loomed up. He tried to look ahead, but could see nothing.

Then, suddenly, the torrent thinned, and stopped. He looked up, and through his stinging, running eyes, saw the helicopter climbing away. He looked around. The whole boat was covered in a thick layer of orange sludge.

He went down below, stuck his head inside the shower, and turned it full on, keeping his eyes open. He heard the blast of a horn, then another blast. Dabbing his eyes with a towel, he pushed open the forward hatch and looked out. They were drifting, sideways, right in the path of an enormous rusting barge, towing another, laden with flattened scrap cars. He ran back to the stern, started the engine, and rammed the gear into full reverse.

The boat began to move backwards, then suddenly, the engine began labouring. He pulled the throttle harder back, but the speed would not increase. They were still reversing, but only perceptibly. The freight barge gave several angry blasts, as it bore down, unable to stop, and Lomax tugged frantically at the throttle, throwing it into forward gear, then ramming it back into reverse once more. He saw the temperature gauge beginning to climb, and realised that the propeller had fouled something.

Somehow, *Harmony* managed to reverse enough to let the barge get past.

'What you fuggin' playin at?' shouted the bargee, angrily.

'Propellor!' shouted Lomax.

'Fuggin' trippers – why don't you stay in the paddlin' pool,' shouted the bargee.

Lomax limped his boat to the shore, and secured her to a couple of trees. Then he went below, lifted the propellor hatch, and reached down into the murky water. An old hosepipe was wrapped around the propellor, so tightly it could scarcely turn. Fuming with anger, at the helicopter, at the people who used the canals as rubbish tips, at everything, he began slowly to unwind the rubber tubing.

It took him two hours to free the propellor, and clean the chemical insecticide off the boat. He had a raging headache, and felt violently sick, probably, he knew, from inhaling the stuff. He heard a helicopter in the sky again, and looked up anxiously, ready to run for cover, but it did not come near this time. He started the engine, and set off, ignoring the speed limit himself this time. He looked up at the sky again, scanning it carefully with his eyes, listening hard. Kenny and his mob were going to be playing at The Welldiggers tonight. Their gear was on the hulk. That meant, almost certainly, they would travel on the hulk.

Lomax slowed as he approached a tunnel under the motorway. In the centre of the tunnel, it was pitch dark. As he came out into the bright sunshine again, he slowed down, stopped, and then reversed back through the tunnel, heading for an inlet he had spotted a short distance back.

CHAPTER TWENTY-ONE

Len Martin sat behind his desk, drumming his stubby fingers as he thought hard. He had a large frame, athletic, but ruined by a massive beer gut, and a blunt face, with close-cropped hair brushed forward, giving him something of the appearance of a small-time football coach.

'Martin Coaches,' said the voice of his secretary/receptionist, through the thin wall of the prefab building. Outside, he heard the roar of a diesel engine rise and fade, rise and fade; it began to irritate him. For half an hour it had been doing the same, rise and fade, rise and fade. Surely to God they must have found the problem by now?

He tugged a pack of King Edward cigars out of his pocket, dug his thumbnail into the cellophane, and ripped it across. There was a knock on the door.

'Yeah?'

The door opened, and in walked a tall, thin man. His back was ramrod straight, and he walked stiffly. 'Ready, boss,' he said.

'About bloody time. Engine all right, Johnny?'

'Fine,' said the coach driver, Johnny Goff.

'You sure your back's going to be all right?'

'Clean bill of health,' said Goff.

'Don't want one of your discs flying out on this run.'

'I'll be fine.'

Martin nodded. 'Don't forget the French cops do "on the spots" – can look at your tach, and say "You go too fast, m'sieur, you pay 600 francs."'

'I'll remember.'

'You get fined, you pay. Right?'

'Fair enough.'

'And you have to carry a guide in Paris. One per coach.'

'French like mine, I'll need a guide.'

'Any problems, Bonnard'll sort them out.' He paused, lit his cigar and inhaled deeply. 'And don't forget the duty frees, eh?' he said, giving Goff a knowing look.

Goff smiled, and walked stiffly out. There was a buzz on Martin's intercom. He pressed the switch.

'Yeah?'

'There's a Mr Pember here to see you.'

'What?' said Martin, angrily. 'Send him in.'

Pember walked into the office, and shut the door behind him.

'What the fuck you doing here, you berk? I told you never to come here.'

Pember looked at him guiltily. 'I was passing – safer than using the phone.' Pember wrung his hands together. 'He's still here.'

'You tit,' said Martin. 'You stupid tit. It's coincidence, I told you, that's all. Got a narrowboat. Canals are his home.'

'But why here?'

'Jesus. Why anywhere? You're cracking, Pember, you're bloody cracking. You're going to lead him straight to you, you know that? If you'd just left him alone, done nothing – what could he have done? Nothing. Know what you're doing, don't you?'

Pember glared at him. 'What do you mean?'

'What do I mean? You're drawing attention to yourself; everything you do. I told you to leave him alone. Instead, what do you do, you lay a bloody spiv on him to burn his broad and his boat.'

'It was a diversion; a smokescreen.'

'Yeah; bloody smokescreen all right. Too bloody right. You're off your bloody rocker.'

Pember pulled up a chair and sat down angrily. 'Naylor went too far; that was the problem.'

'Brilliant act, he did. Where d'you get him from?

Opportunity Knocks?'

Pember stared at him in silence. 'The idea was to put Lomax off the scent.'

'He wasn't on any scent.'

'Lomax is no fool. I wanted him to think that the underworld was looking for the loot. Give him the impression they'd checked out everyone else, so he wouldn't suspect any of the others – from the Squad.'

Martin shook his head. 'You're a messer; a right fucking messer.'

'Naylor's dead now. Dead men don't talk.'

'Not worried about them when they're dead, Pember. It's what they say when they're alive that's the problem. Know what I mean?' he said, knowingly. 'What they do when they're alive. And what they don't do. Promises they don't keep.' He leaned forward, and grabbed the neck of Pember's shirt, shaking him violently.

'I was a copper,' said Pember. 'You'd better not forget that, Martin, or I'll lay you out cold.'

Martin looked at him hard, for a moment, then realised he meant it. He released his grip, contemptuously. 'Yeah; keep forgetting you were a copper. I reckon Lomax got more influence in the police force than you have.'

'They couldn't bust him. They couldn't find anything.'

'Maybe Lomax gave them a bigger cheque than you did? Ever think of that, Pember?'

'I've got the local heavies on him now,' said Pember. 'They'll move him. They'll move him a long way.'

'Local heavies? Who you got? Mickey Mouse or Donald Duck? You're a fucking messer, you know that? Everything you do, mess, mess, mess. Million quid's worth of smack there was on that deal. Did we get that? We got the fucking peanuts. You said you'd get someone to lose him in jail. No one did. Now he's out, you can't even move him on anywhere.'

'These people will.'

'Leave him alone, Pember, I'm telling you. More you push him, more suspicious he's going to get. If he finds out you're behind it all, then he's going to twig. Then you're going to be in trouble. And me. Big trouble.' Martin drew heavily on his cigar. 'Now piss off, I'm busy – and don't you ever come here again.'

Pember got up and walked towards the door. He turned back to Martin. 'Making a big mistake, if we don't move him on.'

'I only made one mistake: getting involved with you in the first place.' Martin took a drag of his cigar, then tore it away, and blew the smoke out of his mouth as if it were a piece of food that was off. 'They ever get you in court, they'll melt the keys.'

'They get me in court, you'll be sitting right beside me. That's a promise.' Pember slammed the door shut behind him.

Martin sat and stared at the door for some minutes, then he pulled open a drawer, and lifted out his address book. He flicked through the pages, until he found the number he was looking for. He lifted the phone, and punched out the number. After a few rings it answered.

'Charlie?' he said. 'Len Martin.' He paused. 'Yeah, fine. Yeah, she's fine. Hasn't lost her knack of spending money. Yeah, kids are fine too.' He paused again. 'That special service you have – still running it? Yeah, that's the one. I want someone. Pro. Real pro, know what I mean?' He paused again. 'Cheshire,' he said. 'Lives alone.' He paused again. 'Yeah, soon as you like – yeah – could meet you tomorrow morning.' Martin tapped the ash off his cigar and began to smile.

CHAPTER TWENTY-TWO

It was shortly before five-thirty when Lomax heard the blattering of an unsilenced engine. He looked up from the dark shadow of the tunnel, and saw the familiar battered hulk rounding the corner.

He stood up and flattened himself against the wall. He would be invisible, he knew, to anyone coming in from the bright light. Travelling at four miles per hour, the barge would be in the tunnel for about forty-five seconds. It all depended on where Kenny was. As the barge drew closer, he smiled. Kenny was on his own, at the tiller. The purple-haired youth was sitting on the roof, near the front, reading; no one else was on deck.

He knelt down and picked up the heavy chunk of driftwood he had plucked out of the canal earlier, and waited, watching.

The noise of the exhaust began to echo, as the hulk entered the tunnel. He could see the figures clearly, still, the purple-haired youth putting his book on his lap. The tunnel was only just wider than the hulk; there was no danger that the hulk would be too far out from the bank. The nose of the boat slipped past him, then the dark shadow of the youth on the roof. Lomax waited a few seconds longer. Now!

With his left hand, he grabbed the rear protective rail of the hulk, and leaped on to the stern. He brought the blunt end of the wood crashing down on to the back of Kenny's head, and the scouse slumped over without a sound. Lomax bent down, put one arm under his knees, one under his back, and hoisted him, unsteadily and with difficulty, up.

Then he leaned over the side rail, and pushed him, as hard as he could, praying he would land on the embankment, and not splash into the water. He heard a dull thud, and jumped ashore himself, landing right on top of Kenny, and crashing to the ground. He looked around, and watched the stern of the barge slipping serenely out into the light at the far end.

He hoisted Kenny in a fireman's lift, ran as fast as he could, in a stooped, stumbling run, out of the tunnel, through the fencing at the side, well concealed by several trees and a hedgerow, up towards the deserted mill he had found earlier that afternoon.

He pushed open the rotting door, and dropped the scouse on the floor. A cloud of dust shot up all around him. He lifted Kenny up by his armpits, dragged him across the floor, and propped him against the wall. He saw a length of cord on the floor, in a corner, and bound Kenny's hands together tightly. Then he picked up an old pail, went over to a tap, and turned it on. There was a hiss of air, then rust-coloured water began to spew out. He took the pail back, and threw it over Kenny's face.

Spluttering, the scouse shook his head a couple of times, like a dog. He looked around, confused, looked up at Lomax, then looked around again.

'Nice snooze?' said Lomax.

'Whasshappening?'

'Not a lot.' Lomax walked over to Kenny, and unbuckled the massive studded belt he was wearing. Slowly, and menacingly, Lomax wound it around his fist, making a massive knuckle-duster. He smiled at Kenny, then hurled a vicious punch into the wooden beam beside his head. Dust and splinters showered on to Kenny's face.

Lomax looked at the belt, and picked a few splinters off the studs. 'Useful belt,' said Lomax. 'Ideal if you want to belt someone, eh? Or do you just use it for keeping up your trousers?'

Kenny glared at him.

'Not in a chatty mood, eh?'

'I've got a headache.'

'Sorry,' said Lomax. 'Forgot my aspirins. Still,' he said, slowly, 'time I've finished with you, you won't be needing aspirins.' He unwound the belt a short distance, and began to swing it around, close to Kenny. ''Bout time you and I had a chat, isn't it? Gone out of your way to make life difficult for me, just lately, haven't you? Untying my boat. All that music. Dope. Fly spray. Regular little bundle of fun, you are; make any party go with a bang. Why you doing all this to me? What have I done to you?'

Kenny stared at him, silently. Lomax crashed another punch into the beam, this time much closer to his head. Kenny flinched.

'Just trying to jog your memory,' smiled Lomax.

'I didn't mean nothing,' said Kenny.

'Oh?' said Lomax, feigning surprise. 'How's that?'

Kenny shrugged.

Lomax slammed in another punch, this time clipping his ear. Kenny screamed, a mixture of pain and fear.

'Like one of those in the balls?' said Lomax.

'No,' he said, fearful. 'No, no.'

'I won't hit you there – not as long as you keep talking.'

Kenny looked at him again. 'Someone wants you moved on.'

'Don't know anyone called "Someone",' said Lomax. He aimed his fist at Kenny's crutch.

'I don't know why,' he screamed.

'Who? I said **who**? Not **why**? **Who?**'

'Dunno.'

'You usually take on jobs from people whose names you don't know?'

'I didn't want to know his bloody name.'

'How much is he paying you?'

'Two-fifty.'

'My, my, you do come cheap. Maybe you'd like to describe him?'

'He's local.'

'No? Never!'

'Bill. He's Bill – or ex-Bill.'

'How do you know?'

'You can tell, can't you?'

'And he gave you the pot, eh?'

Kenny nodded.

'He into drugs?'

He shrugged.

'Describe him. Face. Hair.'

'Dark hair; quite tall; thin.'

'How'd he find you?'

'Pub. Challenged me to arm wrestling. Burned my fugging hand.' He paused, then spoke again, sullenly. 'I know where he lives.'

'How do you know that?'

'Not stupid, am I? Followed him, didn't I? Wanted to make sure I got me money; the other half.'

'Where does he live?'

Kenny shook his head.

'Memory gone?'

Kenny stared at him sullenly again. 'Funny, you know, Kenny, how you can go off people.' He clicked his finger and thumb together. 'Just like that.' He took a short step over to Kenny. Kenny screamed out in fear. Lomax dragged him backwards again, across the floor, to the centre of the room. A great hook hung above, for raising bales of hay. Lomax unwound the rope, and lowered it down. Kenny watched, fearful. Lomax hitched the hook through the cord binding his hands.

'Like flying, don't you?' said Lomax.

Kenny stared at him, warily.

Lomax gave a violent jerk on a rope, and with a scream of terror, Kenny was hoisted into the air. Lomax pulled again, until Kenny was suspended midway between the floor and the hatch up into the loft, then made the rope fast. 'Don't wriggle it too much. That hook's rusty; don't want it fraying the cords. It's a long drop.'

'Let me down, please let me down.'

'Nice trick, that one of yours this morning – with the helicopter; must tell me where you learned it from sometime,' said Lomax.

'Please let me down, I'll tell you; honest.'

'Don't like being up in the air? You seemed happy enough this morning, in your chopper. Happy as a pig in shit.'

'I'll tell you.'

'Yes,' said Lomax. 'I know you will. See – this mill's deserted. No one comes here. If I shut the door, could be Christmas before you were found.'

'I'll take you there.'

Lomax shook his head. 'Just an address. That's all I need.'

'Dale Park,' he shouted, almost hysterical. 'Daresbury.'

'Thanks,' said Lomax. He walked over towards the door.

'Hey – where you going?'

'Dale Park,' he said, surprised.

'What about me?'

'I want to find out if you're telling the truth. Why don't you hang around for a while?'

'Dale Park, Daresbury,' said Lomax into the receiver.

'Yes,' said Robinson. 'That's Pember's address, definitely. Got problems?'

'Yes. Going to a great deal of trouble to lean on me. A great deal.'

'Interesting,' said Robinson. Very interesting.'

'That's what I thought.'

'Might be worth keeping an eye on him,' said Lomax. 'You might get yourself a good murder story; mine.'

'Still got the obituary, Lomax. Be in the following morning, without fail.' He paused. 'You've only got one middle name, haven't you?'

'Do us a favour, Robbo. Shut up.'

'Just joking.'

'I've already been amused, thanks. Got a new photographer yet?'

'Yes.'

'Suggest you send him up here.'

'What? So you can scare him away?'

'Not this time.'

'Might just do that. Not much happening down here for a change. Beirut quiet. Persian Gulf quiet. Belfast quiet. It's all happening on Britain's inland waterways, eh, Lomax?'

'There's enough happening.'

'Long as no one kidnaps the PM, might be able to lay something on.' He paused. 'Any luck with your kid?'

'Not a dickey. Everyone's seen him. No one knows where he is.'

'Sounds like you should take a lesson from him at the moment.' Robinson paused. 'Oh, by the way. I was sorry to hear about your mother.'

'My mother? Been ill for a long time, I'm afraid.'

'Coming down for the funeral?'

Something in Robinson's voice ran a chill through him. 'Funeral? Well, of course I will,' he said, suddenly irritated. 'When she's dead.'

There was a long pause. 'Perhaps I'm speaking out of turn,' said Robinson, gently. 'Don't you know, then?'

'Know what?'

There was a long pause. 'She died, two days ago, I think it was – someone put the notice on my desk.'

Suddenly, the phone booth seemed to be suffocating him, the walls pressing in all around. Then, they receded, like the tide, and it seemed he could walk for miles and not reach the windows, reach the doors. 'No,' he said, weakly. 'No one told me. I didn't ring in. I – er – I didn't expect it – so soon.' He felt tears brimming into his eyes. 'Thanks for telling me,' he said, weakly.

'Hey, Lomax,' said Robinson. 'I really am sorry; truly sorry. I didn't want to be the one to break the news. Not my business.'

'I'm glad you did, otherwise I wouldn't have known. People can't get in touch with me, you see, unless I phone in.'

'Well, make sure you keep in touch with me,' said Robinson. 'I'll get cracking on Pember. Right away.'

'Thanks,' said Lomax.

But Robinson had already hung up.

CHAPTER TWENTY-THREE

'Man that is born of a woman hath but a short time to live, and is full of misery. He cometh up and is cut down, like a flower; he fleeth as it were a shadow, and never continueth in one stay.'

Lomax stood, hands behind his back, in the small knot of people, faces white, clothes dark, and sodden from the rain that fell incessantly on the North London cemetery.

The vicar spoke, a gentle, firm incantation, like an actor in some bizarre open-air theatre. Lomax stared at the pine coffin that sat on the green Astroturf, watched as the pall-bearers slowly lowered it, expertly manipulating the clean blue tapes. He watched, transfixed. The woman that had borne him was in there. He had lived, once, inside her; inside the lifeless box of flesh and bone that was inside the wooden box. The coffin slid down, out of sight. Gone, he thought to himself; gone, and I never had the chance to tell her. Now, she would never know, he thought bitterly. One moment, you think you have all the time in the world, the next, none. He turned and looked at his father, his body erect, proud, his face stooped forward, taut with grief, struggling to show dignity to the outside world. Lomax looked at him. Perhaps if he had cared a little less about what the outside world thought, and more about what actually mattered, Beatrice Lomax might still be alive, instead of inside that pristine box. 'Shame,' his father had said. 'Shame it was that killed her.'

Shame, thought Lomax bitterly. There was only one shame: that he'd been denied the chance to tell her. Lomax looked around him. He saw something move at the back of the crowd; a small figure; the familiar tossing back of a forelock. 'Christ!' he said. 'Steve!' He spun around, tried to break through the thick wall of people behind him, three of them in a row, his aunts, supported by one of their husbands, locked in grief. He sidestepped around. There was a tangle of people now. Umbrellas popping up. He ducked through them. 'Steve!' he called out. 'Steve!' He ran stumbling. Where? Where? Turned back, looked at the crowd, scanned it closely. He turned on his heels, looked all around. 'No. Don't go. Stay just a moment. One moment.' He scoured the people, the entrance, the gravestones. Nothing. Had he imagined it? No. Impossible. Then where? Where was he? He sprinted across to the church, looked inside. Nothing. People were already arriving for the next funeral. He ran around the back. Nothing. 'Steve!' he shouted. 'Steve!'

He ran out of the gates, scanning the road. Receding into the distance was a bus. Was it possible? There was a car parked; a green Ford Sierra. Two men were sitting in it.

'Did you see a kid leave here? Running?'

'A kid, Lomax?' sneered a voice. 'Cradle-snatching, are we?'

Lomax looked down, to his horror, straight into the smug face of Detective Inspector Sullivan.

'Thought you'd left the smoke, Lomax. Or did you find no one else would have you?'

Lomax eyed the sergeant, who was picking his nose with his little finger.

'My mother's funeral,' said Lomax. 'They let the Kray brothers out of jail to go to their mum's funeral.'

'Compared to you, Lomax, the Krays were saints.' He paused. 'Sorry to hear about your mother, though.'

Lomax stared him back in the eye, waiting for the sting in the sentiment. It came.

'Hear she couldn't face going on living with the knowledge of the son she'd produced.'

'Step out of that car and say that.'

'Tut tut tut, Lomax. This is a funeral. Bit of dignity, eh.

157

Your old man's coming out, right behind you. He wouldn't be too impressed with your having a punch-up at your mother's funeral.'

Lomax stepped back. 'What do you want?'

'Want to see your heels, Lomax, just as soon as you're ready.'

'You'll see them soon enough.'

'Oh – and there's another thing, Lomax.' He paused. Journalist pal of yours. Robinson.'

'What about him?'

'He's making waves.'

'Waves?'

'Yeah. Been going around, interviewing your old cronies. Know what waves do, Lomax?' Sullivan swivelled his hand, up and down. 'They sink things.'

'Really?'

'He's getting in a lot of people's hair, Lomax. Important people. Tell him he should stick to tits and bums. Not good for his health what he's doing right now.'

'He's not my friend and I don't know what he's doing.'

'Word I hear is different, Lomax. Hear you had a cosy lunch together only the other day. Surprised you could spare the time in between knocking off ten-year-olds.'

'Who I have lunch with is none of your business.'

'Oh – we know that, Lomax. We know that, don't we, Sarge? Here, take your finger out of your nose, got a very important man standing here. Most unwanted man in Britain, I'd say.'

'Finished?' said Lomax.

'Your friend Robinson – call him off, eh? It's past. Shouldn't go around sniffing in other people's troughs. It's past; it's happened. People want to forget, Lomax.'

'You don't seem in much hurry to forget.'

'Out of sight, Lomax, out of mind. Soon as you get out of my sight, you'll be out of my mind. Just don't want to go home tonight and find some tit'n'bum man's been raking around in my underwear drawer. Get the message?'

'He could help clear my name.'

'Day he does, they'll make him a member of the Magic Circle. Tell him to lay off.'

'Sounds like a threat, Sullivan.'

'Me? Threaten a journalist? Honourable member of an honourable profession? Oh no.' Sullivan smiled. 'But if for instance his name got dropped off the Commissioner's briefing list... oversights can happen, Lomax. Then where would he be? Eh? Like your Welshman: no good without his leaks.'

'I'll pass it on.'

'You do that, Lomax.' Sullivan turned the ignition key. 'My condolences to your family.' Sullivan accelerated ferociously away.

Later that evening, Lomax sat in the living room of his father's house, in silence. In the armchair opposite him sat his father, staring vacantly into space, beside the coal fire, that was always immaculately prepared throughout the summer, with newspaper at the bottom, neat white sticks of wood, and chunks of coal so black they might have been painted. It was never lit until the autumn.

His father leaned over to the side table, picked up the bottle of Bells whisky, poured a careful two-inch measure, added a further two inches of water, and took a long pull on the drink. He pulled an untipped cigarette from the pack beside him, tapped the end of it on his thumbnail, put it in his mouth, and struck a Swan Vestas. He held the match up, studying the flame for a moment, as if it perhaps contained a hidden message, then held it to the end of his cigarette. He inhaled deeply, and blew the flame out with his exhalation, as was his ritual.

'Eighteen minutes,' said his father, suddenly, bitterly. 'When I was a lad, a funeral meant something. Hour, hour and a half in church. Now it's like bloody McDonalds in there.' He returned to his silence.

'I wish you'd let me see her.'

Ainsley Lomax ignored his son's comment.

'I didn't do it. You won't believe me. But I did not do it. I was framed.'

'Judge was a fair man. If he'd had any doubt, he'd have given you the benefit.'

Lomax glared angrily at his father. 'Come on, Dad. You've been in the Force all your life. How many judges have you seen? How many judges have you ever praised for their verdict?'

The old man drained his glass, picked up the whisky bottle and poured carefully, steadily. When he had finished, he set the bottle down, and held the glass up to study his handiwork. 'Disagreed with sentences, yes. Often. Someone goes out, shoots a policeman; most likely gets one year, with twelve months off for good behaviour. Haven't seen a judge give a proper sentence in twenty years. But the verdict? Haven't seen many give a bad verdict.'

'Rubbish!' shouted Lomax. 'God, I can remember – that raid on the Midland Bank – '74, you told me then, the judge was a lunatic. They were guilty as hell. Shot a teller. And they were acquitted.'

Ainsley Lomax picked up the water jug, and poured into the glass, slowly, steadily. He took another cigarette, and struck another match. 'Get the odd exception,' he said.

'Ever thought that I might be the odd exception?'

'They know. And if they don't know, the police bloody well do. The police were unanimous. The jury was unanimous. The judge was a fair man. Why do you keep trying to deceive yourself? You weren't born honest, that's your trouble.'

'I'm your flesh and blood.'

'Flesh and blood. Flesh and blood. People talk of flesh and blood. We start as one drop of semen, and we go out as a bowl of ash or a box of bones. We're born the way we are and we die the way we are. Did our best for you, and you let us down. End of story.'

'No, it's not the end of the story. Christ, you are so obstinate.'

His father looked at his watch. 'It's been a long day, and I'm tired. I'm not interested in arguing any more.'

Lomax stared angrily at his father. Then he saw a look of immense sadness in the old man's face. He swallowed his reply. His father was right. There was no point in arguing any more.

There was a long silence, broken by a sudden loud clunk, which made his father jump, and look nervously around him.

'Boiler switching on,' said Lomax.

His father nodded.

'You going to be all right, Dad, here on your own?' he said, trying to be kind for a moment.

His father nodded. 'Be lonely, but I'll be all right. Liked home, your mother did.' Suddenly the old man smiled, a sad, bleak smile. 'Couple of summers ago ... maybe more ... we went to Eastbourne. For the day. We sat on the front – deckchairs near the bandstand – with all the other geriatrics. She suddenly reaches over and squeezes my hand. I looked at her; said, "Enjoying yourself?" She nodded. Then you know what she said? "I'd just as soon be at home, you know."'

The old man began to laugh at the memory. 'Daft, sometimes, she were. Daft.'

Lomax arrived at his sister's house tired and sad.

'How did it go?' she said.

'It went. It was all right. I suppose.'

'No fights?'

He shrugged. 'No. No fights.'

'I'm glad,' she said. 'Like a drink?'

'What have you got?'

'Sweet sherry.'

He nodded. 'Fine. Anything. Thanks, anyway.'

'What for?' she asked.

'For leaving us alone.'

'It was a good opportunity, having to put the kids to bed. I thought maybe – you and he – maybe you'd patch it up.'

'Not a chance. As far as he's concerned, I'm guilty, and that's that. The judge's verdict was good enough for him.'

'That's what juries and judges are for, Max.'

'Maybe the whole system's up the creek.'

Lomax's brother-in-law, Geoff, came into the room.

'I'll get your drink,' said Karen.

'Lot of people came,' said Geoff.

'Yes,' said Lomax. 'Football and funerals are about the only things that get people out on rainy days.' He paused. 'Thanks for lending me the suit.'

'Good fit,' said Geoff.

Karen came back into the room, handed Lomax his sherry and sat down beside him. 'Don't feel bad about it,' she said. 'Don't blame yourself.'

'I don't,' said Lomax. 'I just wish – I just wish I could have seen her, had a chance to explain. She would have listened. I wish I'd just gone bloody round there last time I was down, marched in.' He took a sip, and winced at the sweetness.

'What good would that have done you? He'd have fought you, you know.'

'I'd have bloody well laid him out.'

'Don't be silly, Max. I can't believe you'd ever hit your own father.'

'He doesn't consider himself to be my father. "One drop of semen," he said, "one drop of semen all those years ago." That's all he thinks of me as.'

'He loves you; deep down. I'm sure of it.'

Lomax smiled bitterly. 'He's got a funny way of showing it.'

'He's hurt; hurt and shaken, and now he's alone.'

'He's feeling lonely at the moment.'

Karen nodded. 'If he ever wanted to move in with us, then he'd be welcome, but I don't think he would.' She smiled. 'Maybe the best thing. He's stuck in his ways. Don't think he'd understand the way we bring kids up these days. Don't think I could bear his incessant smoking either.'

'What are you doing, Max?' said Geoff. 'Working at the moment?'

'No. Had a job – in a pub – standing in for a barmaid who'd gone to have a baby; but she just came back.'

'Pub work's no fun, I shouldn't think.'

'It's all right.'

'Long hours.'

'I'm used to that.'

'You ought to get another career.'

'I want my old one back,' said Lomax.

'You want to go back in the Force?' said Karen.

'It's what I know,' said Lomax.

'Would they ever have you back?'

'If I cleared my name they'd have to.'

'Do you really think you ever will – could – clear your name?'

'I'm working on it. If I stay alive long enough, I might.' He downed the sickly sweet Moroccan sherry, screwing up his face in disgust. 'Tell me. Did either of you see Steve at the funeral?'

'Steve?' said Karen, her voice raised in astonishment.

Lomax nodded.

'Oh, come on, Max. You're obsessed, you know. He wasn't there. I saw everyone.'

'At the back. I saw him. Right at the end. I ran after him, but he'd vanished. Just disappeared.'

'How could he just disappear?'

'There was a bus leaving. Maybe he jumped on.'

'Max, he wasn't there. Geoff – did you see Steve?'

Geoff shook his head. 'No.'

'Max,' she said. 'Forget Steve. I know he's your son; your only child. But you've got to accept, he's grown up a lot. You inside, the divorce, a lot of traumas for him. Kids either cave in or they grow up when they hit traumas like that. Seems like he's taken off; wants his independence. Maybe he's ashamed? Maybe he couldn't take the hassles, wanted to be alone, for a while. He'll come back. But only when he's ready.'

Lomax looked at her. 'He was there today. I saw him.'

She paused. 'Okay. You saw him. Why didn't he come up, throw his arms around you? Why did he run away?'

'Jan made him a Ward of Court. Maybe he's frightened I'll hand him in.' He paused. 'Maybe he's frightened I'll be angry with him.'

Karen sighed. 'You've been through a lot, haven't you?'

'Enough.'

'Why don't you stop fighting everything for a while? Settle down. Get a steady job. Just give yourself time to adjust, back to normal life.'

'Normal life,' he echoed, bitterly. He looked sadly at his sister. 'You don't understand.' He shook his head. 'That's the problem. No one understands.'

After his sister and brother-in-law went to bed, Lomax lay, uncomfortable, on his makeshift bed on the living room floor, his mind whirring.

After an hour, he sat up, and turned on the light. He looked at his watch. It was one o'clock. He picked up the telephone receiver, and asked for Directory Enquiries. Then he dialled the number he was given.

It rang. Ten rings. Fifteen rings. Still he hung on. Twenty rings. A voice. 'Yes? Hello?' Nervous. He recognised it instantly. 'Hello, anyone there?'

'Pember?'

'Speaking. Who is that?'

'Neil Pember, eh?' said Lomax, suddenly feeling very confident.

'What do you want?' The voice was hesitant.

'You know who?'

'I've a fair idea. What do you want?'

'What do I want? Good question, Pember. How about two years of my life, my job, and my family. How's that for openers?'

There was a long silence. When Pember spoke, he tried to sound nonchalant. 'Perhaps we should have a – er – a talk?'

'We are talking.'

'I mean – in person. Face to face.'

'Why not?' said Lomax.

'When – when would suit you?'

'When you least expect me,' said Lomax. He replaced the receiver.

CHAPTER TWENTY-FOUR

Lomax climbed out of the taxi at the small marina, where he had left *Harmony*, late the next morning. The owner, Elsie Farrow, hurried over and intercepted him as he walked through the gate. 'Max,' she said. 'There's a man hanging around, waiting for you. Says he's a friend of yours. Looks a bit of a funny character to me.'

Lomax frowned. 'Where is he?'

'Went to the village for a bit. Said he'd be back.'

Lomax saw, out of the corner of his eye, the figure of Robinson striding towards them. 'That the one?'

She looked around. 'Yes.'

'Thanks, Elsie. He's okay. Just about.'

'Missed you at your sister's,' puffed Robinson, wiping his face with his handkerchief. 'Hoped I'd catch up with you here.' He paused. 'Did it go off all right? The funeral?'

'Yeh,' said Lomax, drily. 'Went off fine. Was a big success.'

Robinson gave him a weak smile, followed by a frown, unsure whether Lomax was being humorous or bitter.

'Want a drink?'

'Wouldn't say no.'

'Let's go on board.'

The walked over to *Harmony*. 'Hang on,' said Lomax, holding Robinson back before he stepped on the boat. Lomax studied the boat carefully. Everything looked the way he had left it. They went on board. Lomax checked two hairs he had concealed across the rear hatch and the cabin door. They were undisturbed. 'Okay,' he said.

Robinson looked at him anxiously.

'Can't be too careful at the moment,' said Lomax. 'Things that go bump in the night, you know.'

'And things that go boom in the day,' said Robinson.

'More or less what I had in mind.'

They went into the saloon, and Robinson sat down.

'Beer? Whisky? Gin?'

'Haven't got any Pimms, have you?'

Lomax looked at him. ''Fraid not.'

Robinson shrugged. 'Doesn't matter. I only drink it so I can say I had a salad for lunch.' He paused. 'Drop of whisky be fine.'

Lomax brought in their drinks and sat down opposite the reporter.

'It's a rough one, your mother's,' said Robinson. 'Remember mine. Cut me up for a long time.'

Lomax nodded.

'You take parents for granted. Don't reckon they will ever die. Then, suddenly, it happens. You realise. You're on your own. You're next in line.' He took a small sip of his whisky.

'Bumped into my old friend Sullivan yesterday,' said Lomax.

'Tom Sullivan – C.I.D.?'

'No less.'

'Not one of your fans,' said Robinson.

'Not one of yours any more either.'

'Never was.' He paused. 'What do you mean "any more"?'

'Seems you've upset him. Rummaging around. "Sticking your nose into other people's troughs" – he has a choice turn of phrase.'

'Watches *The Sweeney* too much on the box,' said Robinson.

'Told me to warn you to take it easy.'

'What did you tell him?'

'Gave him a lecture on the freedom of the Press.' Lomax smiled. 'Don't think he's a great one for the niceties of civilised society.'

'Hear he could be in trouble soon.'

'Oh yes?'

'Makes you look like an amateur.'

'How come?'

'All that snooping that went on over your affair. Quite a few skeletons fell out of quite a few closets.'

'And he's been rumbled?'

'There's whispers. Nothing definite. DPP's got files on twenty-five of them at the moment, including him. Not surprising he's a bit sore. Might all pass over.' He paused. 'Be a pity if it did, though. Make good copy.'

'Good copy, eh?'

'Name of the game.' Robinson sipped his whisky again, and looked around. 'Hiring one of these things myself this summer. For a week. Going up the Caledonian canal. Hoping the Loch Ness Monster'll turn up and eat my missus.'

Lomax grinned.

'Been busy.' Robinson pulled a buff envelope out of his pocket, and handed it to Lomax. 'Open it.'

Lomax looked at the reporter, then opened the envelope, and pulled out a wad of photographs. He looked down at the faces, and recognised them instantly. 'Stratton's aged – losing all his hair. Dean hasn't changed.' He shuffled through them, and stopped when he saw Pember. 'Blimey. Look at that. His gut. What a slob. He's aged ten years. More.'

'I've spoken to all of them – except Pember, so far,' said Robinson.

'And?'

The reporter shook his head. 'Nothing. Clean. If he had an accomplice, it's not one of them.' Robinson paused. 'You sure about the accomplice?'

'I'm not sure about anything,' said Lomax. 'I just don't think he did it on his Jack Jones. Had to have help. Someone.'

'Thought I might go along, have a chat with Pember. See what he has to say for himself. Put the frighteners on him a bit, maybe?'

Lomax nodded.

'It was definitely him behind this Kenny chap?'

'Yes. May have been him too behind the pyromaniac.'

'Can't see that,' said Robinson. 'Doesn't make sense.' He shrugged. But then, it doesn't make sense this Kenny either. What's he trying to do? Move you on? Why? What harm can you do by travelling the canals down this way, working in a pub? What's here that he doesn't want you to find, eh?'

Lomax looked at him. 'That's what I've been thinking.'

'Someone local got a hold on him? Someone he doesn't want you to meet? Or is it just guilt? Nerves?'

Lomax looked down at the photographs. 'Bit grainy some of these,' he said. 'Could have used a slower film – doesn't need so much depth of field.'

'Bit of a photographer yourself, are you?'

'Taken the odd snap in my time.'

'You know, Max, perhaps you ought to go and pay Pember a visit. He's been trying to scare the shit out of you, why don't you go and scare the shit out of him?'

'You're reading my mind.'

'Offer him a deal. Fifty-fifty. We could set up a nice little trap for him.'

Lomax looked at the man. 'You know,' he said, 'for a tits and bum man, you can be really quite smart. Too bad you weren't this smart three years ago.'

'Afraid I always was a bit of a late developer,' said Robinson.

CHAPTER TWENTY-FIVE

The redhead slipped Martin's wet bathing trunks down, over his thighs, gently caressing them, down over his knees, and over his ankles.

She ran her tongue between each of his toes, then up the inside of his right leg, to the knee, then up the inside of his left leg. She then ran her tongue up the inside of his right thigh, and slowly around his crutch.

Martin gripped the side of his deck-chair tightly, squeezed his eyes shut in pleasure, then stole a glance at his watch. An hour and a half before his wife would be back. He opened his eyes, stared for a moment at the lilo floating on his pool, then suddenly jumped back in his chair, with a gasp of unexpected pleasure. The cordless telephone on the ground beside him began to warble.

'Bugger,' he said. 'Hang on.' He leaned over, picked it up, and slid up the aerial. 'Yes?'

'Len? Pember here.'

'I'm busy. Call you back.'

'No wait. It's urgent. I've had a call from Lomax.'

'Jesus.' He sat up violently in the chair. 'Hey – stop doing that a sec.' He paused. 'No, no, Pember – I was talking to the kids. He wants what?'

'To see me,' said Pember.

'What about?'

'Wouldn't say.'

'What you tell him? To go fuck himself?'

'He sounded like he knew something.'

'So he knows something. What can he prove? You berk.

Any time anyone farts, your hair falls out.'

'Says he's coming to see me.'

'When?'

'I don't know. He said, "When I least expect him".'

'What's that meant to mean?'

'I don't know. Middle of the night, he rang me.'

'Listen. Stay there. I'm on my way over.'

Martin jumped out of the Jaguar and stormed into Pember's house. 'I've just about had enough of this, Pember. Fifty fucking grand is too little for all the aggro. I've decided I want another twenty-five.'

Pember stared at him. 'You're joking. I used my money to buy this place.'

'No you didn't. You told me that you paid for this by selling your house in London. Half what you got for that house went on your divorce, the other half bought this place.' Martin tapped his head. 'I remember these things. See, that way you could answer any awkward questions – like about where you suddenly got the money to retire. So you've still got fifty gorillas stashed away, and knowing how chicken-shit scared you are, I wouldn't be surprised if you still haven't done anything with it. I'll bet it's still planted somewhere, somewhere safe, like here, eh, Pember? Well, I'd like another twenty-five now. Wet-nursing fee.'

'Shut up,' said Pember.

'Shut up, eh? Big words. You suddenly come brave again? Because you didn't sound brave an hour ago on the dog. Seems to me that whenever I'm around, you suddenly get brave. Soon as I'm gone, you piss in your pants. Living on your own isn't good for you, Pember; you ought to hire yourself a nanny.'

Pember glared at the man. 'There's a Fleet Street man up in the area.'

'Oh yeah? Who is it? Someone from the woman's page?'

'Robinson. The man who took the most interest at the time.'

Martin frowned. 'What's he doing?'

'I told you. Sniffing around.'

'Then maybe you should break his nose for him. Tell him to go sniff somewhere else.'

'I'm worried. There may be a connection between him and Lomax. Had a bit of a tip-off.'

Martin pulled out a pack of King Edwards, took a cigar, pulled off the cellophane, and lit it. He walked over to the window and looked out at the deserted amusement park, then across at the empty boats, tied up at the edge of the lake. 'What the hell do you do all day long in this place? Fish and jerk yourself off? It's the middle of summer. Where are the punters?'

'Haven't done any advertising.'

'Maybe you ought to start.'

'Don't need to,' said Pember, smugly.

'Oh yeah? What's your sales technique? Telepathy?'

Pember stared at him, and smiled, without humour. 'All my life, smart alecs – like you – have been sneering at me... telling me... not too bright... feet are too big, brain's too small.' He paused. 'Well, you see that hill?' He pointed, and Martin nodded. 'It isn't the Fifth U.S. Cavalry coming over it, its the new motorway.'

Martin looked at him, amazed. 'Through here?'

Pember nodded, smiling less icily now. 'Fill in the lake. Raze the whole bloody place.'

'You're kiddin'.'

'Brother-in-law's the borough architect. Plans are due to be passed next month. I can name my price.'

'That why you came here?'

'Not bad, eh, Martin? Not bad for a jerk?'

'Yeah,' said Martin. He paused. 'You'll be able to think about all that money you could be spending, while you're lying in the prison cell. Fifty-seven are you now? You'll be over sixty before they let you out.' Martin lit his cigar.

'I thought perhaps –' Pember hesitated '– we could pay him off.'

'We?' said Martin. 'We?'

Pember nodded.

'Pay him off. Yeah. Smart idea. I'm all for that, Pember, all for a bit of peace and quiet. All for spending a day in the office without getting a phone call from you panicking 'cause the wind's blown your underpants off the line. Yeah. Pay him off.' He stared at Pember, hard. 'But not we. You.'

'We're in this together, Len.'

'I told you to leave him alone. If you had, nothing would have happened. You didn't do what I said. You can pay the bloody bill.' Martin stared out of the window once more. 'You might be able to get away with a couple of grand. Shouldn't think he's got much dough.'

'He won't come cheap,' said Pember. 'I can tell you that.'

Martin shrugged. 'You'll have to give him what he wants.'

'We,' Pember said, emphatically.

'Afraid all my money's in my coach business,' said Martin.

'And all mine's in here.'

'Bollocks. There's fifty grand in the safe.'

Pember glared at him, marched across to a drinks cabinet, reached in the back of it, and pulled out a key. He walked across the room, and lifted up the thin carpet in one corner, to reveal a small safe in the floor. He unlocked it, and swung up the door. 'Okay, Len, there's the safe. Show me the fifty grand.'

Martin peered in. There was a wad of bank notes, and a birth certificate. Martin pulled out the banknotes, and began to count the money.

Pember sat down, and watched him. When he had finished, Martin looked up.

'Nine and a half grand, I make it.'

Pember nodded.

'Where's the rest.'

Pember opened his arms. 'Like I told you. You're sitting in it. This – and a couple of not-so-good investments.'

'It'll have to do, then, won't it?' Martin shoved the money back in the safe, slammed shut the door, locked it, and handed Pember back the key. 'You'd better invite him round here, show him that. Maybe he'll believe you.'

'Invite him here?' said Pember, nervously.

'Why not?'

'He might attack me.'

Martin tapped his own chest. 'I'll be here.'

'How will you know when he's coming.'

'Easy,' said Martin, grinning. 'We'll invite him.'

CHAPTER TWENTY-SIX

Lomax was smiling to himself. An hour earlier, he had seen Kenny's hulk chug past. The purple-haired youth was on the tiller, and Kenny was sitting in the cockpit, leg in plaster up to his thigh. They had caught each other's eye; but that was all. Neither of them had anything to say to the other any more. He had got Susie to rescue him later on the day he had left him on the hoist. But he must have freed himself and jumped, he thought.

'Oi, mister!'

Lomax looked down from the roof of *Harmony*, at Elsie Farrow's son, or grandson, he wasn't sure, Jamie his name was, who was always hanging around the yard. 'Yes?'

'Got a message for you. From Mr Robinson.'

'What's he say?'

'Told me to tell you to meet him at Pember's place, six o'clock today.'

'Today?' said Lomax.

The boy nodded.

'Six o'clock.'

The boy nodded again.

'What did he look like, Mr Robinson?'

The boy looked at him. 'Old geezer. Had a bow tie.'

Pember nodded. 'Say anything else?'

'No.'

'Thanks.' Lomax looked at his watch, then dipped the brush into the paint pot. What, he wondered, did the wily journalist have up his sleeve? He pulled the brush out and smiled. He looked forward to this evening.

Pember looked at his watch, and then looked anxiously out of the window, just in case. Just in case what, he wondered? In case Lomax arrived early? It was half past five; he was due at six. Where the hell was Martin? He had promised to be here, concealed, in case there was trouble.

Trouble. The word ran around his mind. Yes, of course there would be trouble. Lomax wasn't dropping by to shoot the breeze. For four years they had been partners in the drugs squad. Lomax had never been a great talker, chatterer, never one to shoot the breeze then.

What the hell did he know? he wondered. Bluff. Perhaps it was just bluff. He walked over to the drinks cabinet, unscrewed the top of a bottle of Teachers, began to fill the cap with hands that were shaking so much, he was chucking great drops of the whisky on to the floor. He swallowed the capful down in one gulp, felt the liquid against the back of his throat, then the burning sensation in his stomach. He poured another capful, and downed that, then he screwed the top back on and put the bottle back in the cabinet. He felt a bit better.

Anxiously, he looked out of the window. Martin. Where the hell was Martin? He'd promised to be here, hiding in a back room, just in case. The whisky wasn't doing him much good, he realised, looking at his trembling fingers. He walked over to the hall, picked up his twelve-bore shotgun, moved it from one side of the door to the other. For the umpteenth time, he broke it open, checked that there was a cartridge in each of the barrels, closed it again, and checked that the safety catch was disengaged.

He stood back and looked at the position of the gun. No. He'd see it. Had to be somewhere he could get to it quickly, if trouble started. He wished now he had a pistol, any sort, wished he had nicked one when he had been in the Force; so easy.

Somewhere inside him, he knew, he had been preparing for this day for a long time. He had never really believed he had got away with it. Hoped, yes, always hoped. But it had seemed too easy, gone too smoothly. What the hell did

Lomax know? How was he, after two years in prison? Pissed off, for sure; damned pissed off. But proof? What proof could there be? None. There wasn't any. The tracks had been covered, time and time again; watertight, the whole thing. Relax, he told himself. There is nothing. Nothing to be afraid of. Don't appear nervous, just calm, smile, offer him a drink, invite him into the lounge, tell him how sorry you are about how badly he has been treated by the police, by justice. Offer him sympathy. Help even. Any help he wants.

The thought made him feel better. Of course. Lomax couldn't pin anything on him, so be helpful. That would throw him off his guard. He smiled. He liked that idea. Why the hell had he not thought of it before, he wondered?

He heard a door open, through the kitchen, and fear shot through him, made him jump so hard, the shotgun crashed on to the floor. He picked it up, held it out. 'Who's there?' he said. 'Who's there?' he shouted, louder, conscious of his voice trembling.

The kitchen door to the hallway opened, and out walked a man he had never seen before. He jumped back in surprise, and fear, holding the shotgun out in front of him. 'Who the hell are you?'

'Len Martin asked me to come. He's tied up – got a problem in the office.'

Pember breathed a sigh of relief. He studied the small, thin, neat man, immaculate short hair, face very white, in spite of the fine summer, hands tiny, but beautifully manicured, they could almost have been the hands of a doll. He wore a light anorak and dark trousers, with white moccasins.

'Christ!' said Pember. 'You didn't half give me a shock.'

'Could you – er – stop pointing that thing at me. Making me nervous.'

Pember lowered the gun towards the ground. 'What's wrong with the front door?'

'Didn't want to come in the front way – case I was spotted – you know – case he came early.' The man spoke with a cockney accent. Something didn't quite add up about him,

Pember registered, but he had no time to worry about that now.

'Why didn't you knock? Do you normally come barging into people's houses through their back doors?'

'Bit nervous today, aren't you?'

'A bit? Fucking right, I am.'

The man walked up to Pember and lifted the shotgun away. 'Not crazy about other people's guns.' He paused. 'Jesus. You've been on the bottle. You are in a state, aren't you? You're going to shoot someone.'

'I thought – if there was trouble – might be trouble.'

'That's why I'm here. I'll take care of any trouble.' The man winked at him. 'Know what I mean?' The man broke the gun open, and pulled out the cartridges. 'You open the door to him waving a loaded gun around and there is going to be trouble. Big trouble.'

Pember looked at him, and looked out of the window again. 'Where's your car? I didn't hear it.'

'I was told not to advertise my presence.' The man shoved the shotgun and cartridges into a broom cupboard.

'He's coming,' said Pember. 'Oh Christ. That's him, walking up the drive. You'd better make yourself scarce.'

'And you'd better brush your teeth.'

As Lomax approached the house, he saw a shadow of movement behind a downstairs window. His arrival had not gone unnoticed.

Pember had sounded nervous on the telephone. Frightened. He remembered him as a weak man; a bully boy. Happy to kick terrified homosexuals up against urinal walls, but always happy to let someone else go in front when bursting into the unknown, such as a suspect apartment, where there might be an element of real danger – a booby trap, or armed men.

Too clever. Pember was always too clever. Knew the answers to everything that did not matter. A weasel. Yes. That was Pember.

Lomax's eyes scanned the grounds, scanned the house,

scanned the empty dodgems, scanned the lake. He had waited outside for Robinson for some while, but there had been no sign of him. He assumed Robinson had already gone in. Quite why Robinson wanted him present, he was not sure, but in any event, it suited him well to have a witness to anything Pember might say.

Lomax's eyes never stopped moving, from side to side. He was ready to jump in any direction, dive in any direction, run in any direction.

He rang the doorbell, and again, looked around him.

The door opened. 'Max!' Pember was there, mouth all smiles, terror in his eyes. Big limp handshake, a tang of freshmint, and a blast of alcohol.

'Fine, Neil. Yourself?'

'Mustn't grumble. Come in. Have a drink.'

Lomax thought for an instant that he detected a sideways glance from Pember, at something over to his left. Lomax shot a glance in the same direction, but could see nothing.

'Whisky, if I remember? Ice and water?'

'Just have a glass of water. The nick gets drinking out of your system,' he said, harshly.

'Perrier?'

'Trent and Mersey tap'll do fine. Like to keep it patriotic.'

A smile tried to break out on Pember's face. It just failed. 'Come through. Bit of a mess I'm afraid. Janet used to be the tidy one.'

'You still together?'

'I wanted to live in the country. She wanted to live in the Smoke,' said Pember, from the kitchen.

Lomax heard the sound of a tap running. 'How're the kids?'

'Son's in the merchant navy. Melanie's married a New Zealander. Gone out there.'

Lomax glanced around. The place was functional. Mats; boots; a few prints on the wall, chosen to hide cracks rather than from any love of art. He wondered whether to say anything about Robinson. He decided not to. Perhaps Robinson was already here, hiding somewhere? 'Nice place you got here. Butlins better watch out. When do you open? In the winter?'

Pember came out of the kitchen carrying a glass of water and a glass of whisky. He handed Lomax his water, and led him through into the lounge.

'Blighted at the moment. Equipment needs a lot of work on it. No point spending the money till the council's made up its mind.' He paused, and took a long pull on his drink. 'Sorry – Alan – you know – really sorry about all your troubles. Never believed you were guilty, you know. None of the lads did.' He shrugged his shoulders. 'Terrible business.'

Lomax stared at him. 'Cut the crap, Pember.'

Pember lowered his glass from his lips, and he lowered his head slightly, so that he had to raise his eyes upwards to see Lomax.

'You believed I was innocent, did you, Pember? Well, you must have a bloody short memory, because you didn't tell the judge that, did you? Why not? Did you forget, while you were standing up in that dock? Is that what happened?'

Pember stared at him, anxiously.

'Funny, Pember, you didn't forget anything else. Didn't forget any of the other details, did you? You even remembered what time I'd had a piss three weeks before. And yet you forgot to tell the judge you reckoned I was innocent?'

'We weren't asked to give opinions, Max. Only facts. I thought the facts would help you – don't you see? I thought you were innocent, so, by giving the facts, I thought they would be bound to prove your innocence.'

'Pember – someone telephoned my newsagent, said it was me; ordered fifty copies of the *Standard* to be delivered to my door. Funny, isn't it, how you remember little things in life; trivial things, know what I mean?'

Pember stared at him.

'Like a week before that order was placed, we were sitting in the car one day, driving along, Chalk Farm Road it was, you told me there was some friend of yours moving into my neighbourhood, and did I know a good newsagent? Trivial,

179

isn't it.' Lomax smiled, and watched Pember go puce.

'What do you want, Max?' he said, coldly.

'Me? Want? You know what I want. I want to clear my name. I want compensation for two years of my life pissed down the drain in the nick. I want my job back. I want my son back. All right for openers?'

'I'll help you any way I can,' said Pember. 'Course I will. Give any evidence you want.'

'Leave off, Pember. Evidence? From you? I'd sooner have Dr Crippen as a character witness than you.'

Pember sipped his drink again, and looked down. The glass was empty. Pember put it down. 'How much do you want?'

'How much? How much what?'

'Money.'

'Hundred grand, Pember.'

'What?'

'You heard.'

'You're mad.'

Lomax shook his head. 'I want it returned, Pember. To its rightful owners. The Metropolitan Police Force.'

'You are mad.'

'No, Pember. Quite sane. You see, it's simple. Either you return that money, or I'm going to kill you. I don't like having my girlfriends set on fire. I don't like having drugs planted on my boat. And you know what I really don't like, Pember?'

Pember stared silently back at him.

'I don't like being sprayed with pesticide.' Lomax saw Pember's eyes look upwards for a brief second. Instinctively, he began to move, but too late to avoid the punch that slammed into the back of his neck.

'What the hell did you do that for?' said Pember, furious.

'My hands must have slipped,' said the man Martin had sent. He turned Lomax's head over. 'Won't be out long. Five minutes – ten at the most.'

'That was stupid.' Pember glared at him. 'Now what are we going to do?'

The man smiled at him. Something about the smile made Pember go cold with fear. He stared at his face, then looked down at his hands. He saw the muzzle of the silenced automatic pointing at him. He shook his head. 'No,' he said. 'No! We could do a deal. You and I –'

Pember shrieked as the bullet slammed into his chest, flinging him upwards and sideways across the arm of his chair.

The man knelt down, picked up the unconscious Lomax, pulled him on to the sofa, squeezed his fingers around the trigger of the gun, aimed the gun at Pember, who was staring in horror, unable to move, opening his mouth, trying to speak, and squeezed the trigger again. The bullet tore into Pember's forehead, an inch above his nose, snapping his head back, and down on to the cushion.

He took the gun out of Lomax's hand, wiped it carefully with his handkerchief, then pulled on a pair of gloves. He put the gun back into Lomax's hand, and carefully entwined Lomax's fingers around it.

Next he walked over to the drinks cabinet, felt around inside it, removed the key to the safe. He walked over to the corner of the room, where Martin had told him, lifted the carpet, and found the safe. He unblocked it, and swung the door up. He removed the banknotes, walked across the room, and crammed them into Lomax's pockets.

Then he walked over to the telephone, picked it up and dialled 999.

'Police,' he hissed to the operator.

There were several clicks, then a voice said 'Police.'

'Help me,' he hissed. 'Help me. Dale Park. Daresbury.' Then he forced the telephone into Pember's hand, pulled the fingers around it.

'Hello, caller?' he heard the voice, sounding a long way away. 'Hello, caller?'

He pulled the phone out of Pember's hand, and put it back on the hook.

Then he went over to Lomax, and slapped Lomax's face, gently, first one cheek, then the other. Lomax mumbled, incoherently. The man glanced around the room once more, then slipped out through the kitchen, and began to run, the concealed back route out of the estate. Pember's own escape route, he had once told Martin, in a moment of weakness induced by drink, in case any one should ever 'come' for him.

Somewhere in the distance, as he reached his own safely-concealed car, he heard the shrieking of a police siren.

CHAPTER TWENTY-SEVEN

Lomax was vaguely aware of the slamming of a door. He opened his eyes, but nothing would focus. He felt dizzy, closed them again. Something hot pressed against his thigh. Tried to move his hands; heavy as lead; his right one heaviest of the two. A siren, somewhere, getting louder. Must be near a main road. Near a hospital? His mind rambled. Taking his mother to hospital? He opened his eyes again. Still the blur. Someone asleep in the chair opposite. Father. Nodding off whilst talking to him. The siren stopped. The ambulance. Must let them in.

He stood up, and fell flat on his face. Stood up again; right arm was heavy, so heavy. The door opened. Two men standing there. They froze, looked at him. He looked back. Ambulance drivers? Wrong uniform. He knew the uniform, knew it well. What the hell was it?

One of the men suddenly dived to the ground, and Lomax felt himself being flung backwards. A great heavy weight descended on him, pinioned down his chest to the ground, something smashed into his wrist, hurt like hell.

'Don't move,' the voices said. 'Don't move,' they repeated.

He was rolled over on to his stomach, arms yanked behind his back. Something pinched his wrists tight, something cold, metallic. He smelt dust from the carpet, heard the dripping of water. Water running down the sleeping figure opposite in the chair. Not his father. He began, suddenly to wake up fast. Too fast. Not water. Blood. Pember. Hole in his forehead. Blood down his face. Eyes open, motionless.

He was jerked to his feet, slammed up against a wall.

Hands patted him, down his back, stomach, up between his legs, patted his jacket. He was spun around. One of the policeman was talking into a radio now.

The other patted his jacket pocket, pulled out a wad of banknotes, patted the other pocket, pulled out another wad. Lomax watched, helplessly, speechlessly, trying to put the pieces together through his splitting head.

'Name?'

'Lomax.'

The man tugged his wallet out from his breast pocket, flicked it open, looked at the driving licence, closed it and put it back.

'You're under arrest, Mr Lomax. I caution you that anything you say may be taken down and used in evidence. You don't have to say anything.'

'It's all right,' said Lomax, wearily, falteringly. 'I – er – I know the routine.'

He heard the sound of retching, turned around, saw the other policeman, just a boy in his teens, he realised, leaning out of the window, puking. He heard a second siren, and then a third. One siren approached much faster than the other. Heard the roar of an engine, squeal of brakes, ratchet of a handbrake, car door slam, footsteps, and Dectective Inspector Jakeman was standing in the room, with a grim look on his face. 'Well, well,' he said. 'So we meet again, Mr Lomax. Stopped playing with jamjars, have we?'

'You must have known he had money there.'

'How?'

'Come on, Lomax, I wasn't born yesterday.'

He was enjoying it, thought Lomax, bitterly. The bastard. He looked around the Police Station interview room. Like any interview room. Small. Airless. Formica-topped table. Utility chairs.

'I'm in no hurry, Lomax.'

The headache was acute still, and Lomax looked at his watch. Eleven o'clock. Jakeman had come in, gone out. Come in again, gone out again. Questions. The same ones.

Over and over.

'Nice gun. Where d'you nick that from?'

'What gun?'

'The one you shot Pember with.'

'I didn't shoot Pember.'

'Suicide, was it? Couldn't stand talking to you any longer? Was that it? Suppose anything's possible, eh, Lomax – when you're around?'

'Very funny.'

'Funny? Very funny?' Jakeman scribbled on his notepad, and smiled. 'Judge'll like that. Jury'll like that. Go down well, that will.'

'Why don't you go screw yourself, Jakeman?'

'Detective Inspector – or Sir, to you.' Jakeman paused. 'Like to get everyone to do their own work, do you, Lomax? People to kill themselves? People to screw themselves? You're taking the new leisure society a bit too literally, aren't you? Perhaps you've spent too long in nick, eh? Lost touch with reality? Still, good practice, spending time in nick, because you're going to spend a long long time there in the future, so you might as well get in practice now.' He leaned forward. 'Your two-year stretch, that you just did. That's going to seem like a holiday camp compared to where you'll be going. Do you know that, Lomax? A holiday camp.'

Lomax lay on his bunk the following morning, and listened to footsteps walking down the corridor outside his cell. He cursed himself for having been so stupid, for not having double checked with Robinson. But how could he have done, he wondered? He hadn't known where he was. All night, his brain had raced backwards and forwards through the events of the past day. The walk up Pember's drive. The sideways glance of his eyes.

The footsteps stopped outside the cell, and a voice called out: 'Lomax?' It was Jakeman's voice.

Wearily, Lomax stood up and walked to the door. He saw Jakeman's leering face through the bars.

'Comfy night, eh, Lomax? Home from home?'

'What do you want?'

'Kid named Steve. Belong to you?'

Lomax stared at him, wondering what was coming next. 'Yes.'

Jakeman nodded, slowly. 'Never had a father and son in here together, before. Have to be separate cells of course; police rules.'

'Have you found him? Where is he?'

'Lost him, have you, Lomax? Very careless of you.' He paused, and leaned a little closer. 'Convenient, though. I wouldn't want to go around admitting he was my boy, either.'

'What are you talking about, Inspector Jakeman?'

'We've had tabs on a Steve Lomax, for some while,' said Jakeman. 'Dope merchant. Doing very nicely. 'Fraid we're about to queer his patch in a big way. In a few days. Thought to myself, Lomax – now that's a familiar name – familiar name for trouble – know what I mean?'

'Drugs?' said Lomax. 'Impossible. You bastard – you're setting him up,' he shouted.

Jakeman shook his head and smiled. 'Doesn't need no setting up. Not him. Nor his chums.'

'Let me talk to him,' said Lomax.

'Sure, Lomax, of course. What you want to tell him about? Prison life, eh? Father to son tips on how to cope?'

Lomax stared at Jakeman. 'One day, Jakeman. One day you'll be sorry.'

'Sorry now,' he said. 'Sorry I ever heard the name Lomax.' Jakeman turned and walked away.

Lomax sat down on his bunk again, and stared blankly at the wall. Was it true? Was it possible? Sadly, he knew all too well it was. He had to get out of here, had to find Steve, find him fast, before the police arrested him. From what Jakeman said, he hadn't much time.

His brain began to race, confused. Steve; the events of the previous day. Suddenly, he heard the rattle of a key in the lock. The door swung open, and in walked Robinson, sporting a yellow and white polka-dot bow tie.

'Well,' said Robinson, breezily. 'Here we are again, two

years on, eh?' He pulled up the chair and sat down, then shook his head, sadly. 'Nothing changes, does it, Lomax?'

'There's a limit to how many ways you can decorate a cell,' said Lomax. 'You can either have the bars running horizontal – or vertical.'

Robinson smiled. 'What on earth prompted you to turn up at Pember's place?'

'What do you mean, what prompted me? Your message.'

Robinson stared at him. 'I never sent any message.'

Lomax smiled, weakly, and nodded. 'That's what I've realised. Now.' Lomax gave a short laugh, and looked at Robinson. 'I've been stitched again, stitched but good this time.'

'Funny place to buy,' said Robinson. 'An amusement park, boating lake. I'd like to live up here, when I retire. But I wouldn't buy that sort of a place.' He paused. 'Be coming on the market, though, no doubt.' He nodded again. 'Always did like this part of the world.'

'That what you dropped by to tell me? That you're going to be my neighbour? Because if you want to be my neighbour, you'd better start looking for a plot on Dartmoor.'

Robinson looked pained. 'Came to do a little business. Thought you might be in the mood.'

'You thought wrong.'

'Don't get so steamed up, bad for the heart; end up in an early grave.'

'I already did.'

Robinson opened his briefcase, and pulled out a large brown envelope. He handed it to Lomax.

'What's this? My obituary?'

'Don't flatter yourself. It won't be that big.'

Lomax ripped open the sealed top, and pulled out a sheaf of neatly typed sheets of paper, bound together with a small red cardboard triangle at the top, and a thin red cord.

'What the hell's this, Robinson?'

'A contract,' he said, calmly

'Contract?'

187

'Between the paper and yourself.'

'What the hell for?'

'Everything. Your life story. Whole works; warts and all.'

'You got a terrific sense of timing, Robinson. Anyone ever tell you that?'

Robinson pulled another brown envelope from his briefcase. A smaller envelope. He handed it to Lomax.

'You know, Robinson,' he said. 'You're a regular brown envelope freak.'

Robinson smiled.

'Get your mail at home in plain brown envelopes, do you? Wife ever get curious? Postman? Probably reckon you're a bit of a perv, don't they? Bondage? Rubber? Your mail delivery's probably the talk of the street.'

'Only thing that's the talk of any street at the moment is your arrest. Open it. Have a look.'

Lomax looked at him, dubiously, and slipped his hand in the top of the envelope. 'What's in here? Photographs, feels like. Some nice crumpet, eh? Cheer me up?'

Robinson smiled, silently, and watched

Lomax pulled out the photographs, and stared impassively at the first one. It showed a man Lomax had not seen before, taking a package out of the boot of a Vauxhall Cavalier. The next photo, a close up, showed the man taking a gun out of the package, and the third photo, slipping the gun inside his jacket. A further series of photographs showed him walking up to Pember's house, and then running away from it.

'When were these taken?'

'Some of them shortly before you arrived. The others, after Pember was shot.' He paused, and pulled yet another brown package, even smaller, out of the case. 'This is even better.' He handed it to Lomax.

Lomax tore it open, and up-ended it. Out slid a cassette cartridge. He looked quizzically at Robinson.

'Excerpts,' said Robinson. 'The best bits; know what I mean?' He smiled, slyly.

'Thank you,' said Lomax.

Robinson shrugged, and opened the contract at the last page, and tapped his finger on the dotted line at the bottom.

'Your John Henry – along there.'

'This is blackmail, Robinson.'

Robinson adjusted his bow tie. 'Could call it that, I suppose.'

'How quickly will I get out?'

'Had a word with our paper's legal advisors. Could have you out within a day – from when you sign.'

'Got a pen?' said Lomax resignedly.

'Thought you might see it my way,' said Robinson.

'Jakeman won't be happy.'

Robinson sighed, and shrugged his shoulders. 'You can't please everyone.'